Summer Fun?

Stephanie grinned. "I'm going to start on my new, cool image right away."

"How are you going to do that?" Allie asked.

At that moment, Rick left the lifeguard chair and walked around the edge of the pool. He was so cute!

Stephanie stood up and smoothed her blue one-piece suit. "I'm going to meet Rick. I'll dive into the pool, and then ask him for pointers on diving."

"Good luck," Darcy told her.

Stephanie stood and strolled toward the edge of the pool.

She stopped a few steps away from Rick.

You're a good diver. You can do this! she told herself. *Just don't panic.*

Stephanie took a deep breath. She tensed her muscles and took a few steps, getting ready to plunge gracefully into the water.

Tweeeeeeet!

A whistle blew loudly, right behind her. "No running at the pool!" a voice yelled.

Stephanie froze.

She'd know that voice anywhere. But it *couldn't* be!

FULL HOUSE™: Stephanie novels

Phone Call from a Flamingo
The Boy-Oh-Boy Next Door
Twin Troubles
Hip Hop Till You Drop
Here Comes the Brand-New Me
The Secret's Out
Daddy's Not-So-Little Girl
P.S. Friends Forever
Getting Even with the Flamingoes
The Dude of My Dreams
Back-to-School Cool
Picture Me Famous
Two-for-One Christmas Fun
The Big Fix-up Mix-up
Ten Ways to Wreck a Date
Wish Upon a VCR
Doubles or Nothing
Sugar and Spice Advice
Never Trust a Flamingo
The Truth About Boys
Crazy About the Future

Available from MINSTREL Books

Full House™
Club Stephanie

Fun, Sun, and Flamingoes

**Based on the hit Warner Bros.
TV series**

Janet Quin-Harkin

A Parachute Press Book

READING

A MINSTREL® BOOK

Published by POCKET BOOKS

New York   London   Toronto   Sydney   Tokyo   Singapore

A MINSTREL PAPERBACK *Original*

A Minstrel Book published by
POCKET BOOKS, a division of Simon & Schuster Inc.
1230 Avenue of the Americas, New York, NY 10020

A PARACHUTE PRESS BOOK

READING Copyright © and ™ 1997 by Warner Bros.

ISBN: 0-671-00826-9

First Minstrel Books printing June 1997

10 9 8 7 6 5 4 3 2 1

Cover photo by Schultz Photography

Printed in the U.S.A.

Fun, Sun, and Flamingoes

CHAPTER
1

♦ ◂ ◆ ♦

"Only two hours and thirty-five minutes left to the school year!" Stephanie Tanner's blue eyes sparkled as she glanced at her watch. She tucked a strand of her long blond hair into place. "I don't think I can wait that long for summer vacation to begin!" she exclaimed.

"Me either," Allie Taylor answered. "Just think, no more gym."

"No school at all, for almost three whole months," Darcy Powell added. "And we can spend every single day at the pool. I can't wait!"

Allie and Darcy were Stephanie's two best friends. Stephanie had met Allie in kindergarten when the teacher sat them next to each other. They did everything together after that. They had lots in common. They both loved music and books. But Allie could be very quiet and shy—especially around boys.

"Do you realize we can finally go to the pool by ourselves this year?" Allie asked. Her green eyes were bright against the wavy brown hair that framed her face. "I am so excited about it!"

The pool where they belonged had a rule: Children under thirteen must be accompanied by older family members. But this year, Stephanie, Darcy, and Allie were over thirteen—almost fourteen. And they were finally allowed at the pool alone.

"And don't forget what's even more important," Stephanie said.

"What's that?" Allie asked.

"We can *stay* there by ourselves," Stephanie replied.

Allie laughed, then quickly covered her mouth with her hand. She had recently begun to wear braces on her teeth, and she was self-conscious about them.

"It's going to be fantastic," Stephanie added. "Remember last summer at the pool? Every time I tried to talk to a boy, my dad practically chased him away."

"Not this year," Darcy said. "This year, it's no

parents allowed! Just imagine—we can do whatever we want to, when we want."

"And I want to do nothing but lie in the sun and work on my tan," Allie said.

"No way!" Darcy exclaimed. "I'm getting both you guys in shape this summer."

"What are you talking about?" Stephanie asked.

"Swimming," Darcy answered. "I want us all to try out for the San Francisco city swim team next year, remember?"

"We remember. We were trying to forget," Stephanie joked.

"We're not especially good swimmers," Allie pointed out. "Not like you, Darce. You're a great swimmer. Just like you're a great tennis player and a great field hockey player."

Darcy was a great athlete. She was strong and graceful, and she always had energy to spare.

"Really, you guys—being on the team could be lots of fun. You have to join with me." Darcy got down on her knees and clasped her hands together. "Please, please, say you'll try," she begged. She flashed them a wide smile.

Darcy was also wearing braces. But she wasn't the least bit shy about letting them show. Darcy was almost never shy.

Stephanie and Allie laughed. "Okay, okay. We'll try," Stephanie said.

"If you get up off the floor," Allie added.

"Deal!" Darcy leaped up, patting her dark bangs back into place over her forehead. The silver bangle bracelets she often wore clanged together on her wrist. They shone brightly against her dark skin.

"Now I really can't wait for summer to start," Darcy went on. "You'll see—working on your swimming strokes will give you something to look forward to every day. It'll be much better than just hanging out."

"As if anything could be better than that!" Stephanie teased. They had reached Stephanie's locker. She stopped to peer at a piece of folded pink paper that was jammed between the slots on her locker door.

"What's this?" Stephanie pulled the paper out and unfolded it. The front of the paper was covered with fancy writing. She stared at it in surprise.

"Take a look—you won't believe it," she told Darcy and Allie. They peered over Stephanie's shoulder as she read the flyer out loud:

FOR VIPS ONLY
VIP STANDS FOR VERY IN PEOPLE
YOU KNOW WHO YOU ARE!

Under the message was a color picture of a group of girls. They all wore super-stylish outfits in the same shade of pink. Their makeup was perfect, and so was their hair. They looked as if they were fashion models.

"The Flamingoes!" Darcy and Allie exclaimed at the same time.

The Flamingoes were the most popular—and most snobby—group of girls at Stephanie's school. They always wore pink. They did everything together. And they thought they were ultra-cool. And most of the kids at John Muir Middle School agreed!

Stephanie had been asked to join their club once, back in sixth grade. That's when she found out that the Flamingoes couldn't be trusted. They had really wanted to "borrow" Stephanie's dad's phone credit card—to charge all *their* phone calls!

Stephanie had turned them down. The Flamingoes were never friendly to her again. In fact, they went out of their way to be mean to Stephanie and her friends, every chance they got.

Stephanie turned over the flyer and showed the back to Darcy and Allie. They all read it together:

YOU'RE INVITED
TO THE
FLAMINGOES'
END-OF-SCHOOL CELEBRATION
BE THERE.

The Flamingoes had signed their names across the bottom of the page in dark pink ink: Rene Salter, Alyssa Norman, Tiffany Schroeder, Cynthia Hanson, Dominique Dobson, Mary Kelly, Darah Judson, and Tina Brewer.

Stephanie glanced at Darcy and Allie in amazement. "Why are the Flamingoes asking *me* to one of their parties?" she asked.

"They must be up to something nasty," Darcy answered. "Rene Salter has been your worst enemy all year."

"Yeah, ever since Kyle Sullivan asked Steph for a date," Allie added.

"I couldn't help it that Rene liked Kyle, too," Stephanie said.

"I don't think she'll ever forgive you," Darcy added. "I mean, you don't even date Kyle anymore, and Rene is *still* nasty to you."

"Well, don't worry," Stephanie said. "It's almost summer, and I won't be competing with Rene over anything then—especially not a boy. I'm totally glad." Stephanie frowned. "Which is why this invitation makes no sense."

"Maybe Rene wants to make friends now that school's out," Darcy said.

"Yeah, what if it's true?" Allie asked. "And what if you don't go to this party and Rene thinks you're snubbing her?"

"She deserves snubbing," Darcy said.

"But it might make her worse than ever," Allie pointed out.

"How?" Stephanie giggled. "Can you imagine Rene any meaner than she is already?" she asked. "Maybe I should just get rid of this dumb invitation." Stephanie waved the flyer in the air as if she were going to toss it away.

"Hey! Where did you get that?" a sharp voice demanded.

Stephanie knew that voice. She whirled around. Rene Salter was standing right behind her. She was with her best friend, Alyssa Norman.

Rene wore a pink-and-white-checked sundress. Alyssa wore white shorts and a sleeveless pink shirt. Their fingernails gleamed with pink polish, and their pink toenails peeped out of their matching pink patent-leather sandals. Rene's blond hair was parted on one side so that it nearly covered one of her blue eyes. Alyssa's ash blond hair was combed exactly the same way.

"That invitation is for VIPs only," Rene snapped at Stephanie. "Which is definitely not you! Where did you get it, anyway?" she demanded.

"I found it in my locker," Stephanie said.

"In *your* locker? That's impossible!" Rene turned to Alyssa. "How did it *get* there?"

"Don't look at me," Alyssa told her. "I didn't

7

put it there. It must have been Tiffany. I told her to give one to Danielle—her locker is two doors away."

"Tiffany!" Rene rolled her eyes. "Sometimes she is totally clueless!"

Rene snatched the invitation out of Stephanie's hand. "Sorry, Stephanie," she said. "But you should have known this wasn't for you. You guys are the *last* people on earth that we'd invite to one of our parties."

"Don't worry, Rene," Stephanie said in a cool voice. "We're the last people on earth who'd want to *go* to one of your parties."

Allie stifled a giggle. Rene tilted her head and gave Stephanie an icy stare. "Very funny," she said. She turned and headed down the hall. "Come on, Alyssa," she called. "Let's get this invitation to Danielle—where it belongs."

Stephanie watched them go. "I am *so* glad that invitation wasn't for me," she said. "Because that's just one more thing that will be great about this summer." She draped an arm around Allie's and Darcy's shoulders. "We'll have nothing but sun, fun—and *no* Flamingoes!"

CHAPTER
2

♦ ◀ ▪ ♦

Stephanie blinked as bright sunlight shone into her eyes. She sat up with a jolt. Her alarm hadn't gone off! And it was already past eight o'clock!

"Michelle, wake up!" she called across the room to her nine-year-old sister. "We're late for school!"

Wait a minute, she thought. *It's the first day of summer vacation. There is no school!*

Stephanie grinned in delight. She couldn't wait to get started on her summer. She flung off her covers and leaped out of bed. She noticed that Michelle's bed was already empty.

That's weird, Stephanie thought. She often had to drag Michelle out of bed in the morning. *I wonder where she is?* Then Stephanie heard the sound of

9

cartoons blasting from the TV downstairs. She grinned. Michelle was getting a start on her summer, too!

Stephanie hurried down the hall to the bathroom and quickly washed. She combed out her hair, then headed back to her room. She stood for a long time, staring at her closet.

I need to choose the perfect outfit for my first day at the pool, she thought. Finally she decided on her new white shorts and a red Hawaiian-print halter top. She swept her hair up into a ponytail and fastened it with a red scrunchie. She stared at her reflection in the mirror.

Who is that amazing, super-cool girl? she imagined everyone at the pool asking.

"Yeah, right." Stephanie laughed to herself. Still, she *felt* super-cool. Going to the pool on her own was about the most grown-up thing she could imagine.

The pool was part of the local community center. Her family had belonged to the center for years. All the kids in the nearby neighborhoods hung out there. Ever since Stephanie could remember, she had dreamed of being one of the "big" kids. And now it was finally her turn!

She lifted her backpack. Her bathing suit, sunblock, and everything else she needed were already packed inside. She gave her reflection one last glance of approval, then ran downstairs.

"Hey, Michelle. Happy summer!" Stephanie called as she crossed through the living room. Michelle barely looked up from the TV set.

Stephanie pushed through the swinging door to the kitchen. The rest of the Tanner household was already there. Her father, Danny Tanner, was hard at work. He was making pancakes with her aunt Becky. Danny and Becky co-hosted the morning TV show *Wake Up, San Francisco.*

Becky was married to Stephanie's uncle Jesse. Jesse leaned over the table to cut pancakes for their twin sons, Alex and Nicky. The twins were almost five years old.

"More pancakes, Daddy," Nicky called out.

"Sorry, sport," Jesse told him. "These are for Alex."

"Then give me Joey's pancake," Nicky demanded.

Joey Gladstone glanced up from his place at the far end of the table. He grabbed his plate and pretended to hide it from Nicky. "No way!" he exclaimed. "Keep your pancake-begging hands away from me," he teased.

Joey had been Danny's college roommate. He had lived with the family for years, helping Danny raise Stephanie, her older sister, D.J., and Michelle.

"Nicky can have the rest of my pancakes," D.J. told Jesse. "I don't have much appetite."

"Too excited about your first day of work to eat, huh?" Jesse asked.

D.J. nodded. She was nineteen. Her college classes had ended the week before, and she was starting her new summer job today. It was the first real job she'd ever had, working in an office building downtown.

"Hey, Steph, grab a chair," Danny called. "You're next in line for pancakes."

Stephanie slid into her place at the table. The kitchen door swung open and Michelle rushed in, pulling swim goggles over her face.

"Michelle, why are you wearing those to the breakfast table?" Stephanie asked.

"Because I've got my first swimming lesson today. I want to get used to how they feel," Michelle explained.

"Swimming lesson?" Stephanie repeated. "Don't tell me you're going to the pool, too."

"Don't worry," Michelle said. "We're taking swimming lessons at the YMCA Daycamp. Cassie's mom is taking a bunch of us." Cassie was one of Michelle's best friends.

"What a relief!" Stephanie exclaimed. "This is my summer of freedom—the first time ever that

I'm allowed to go to the pool on my own. The last thing I'd need is my little sister hanging around!"

"Don't worry, I don't want to hang around you, either," Michelle said. "Anyway, I'll be too busy with my own friends this summer."

Danny slid a huge stack of pancakes onto Stephanie's plate. "Whoa, Dad! I can't eat all that," Stephanie said. She speared four pancakes with her fork and put them on the twins' plates. They gobbled them up.

"I'm still worried about you hanging around the pool all day, doing nothing," Danny told her. "I think you'll get bored."

"Not a chance, Dad. I'll be very busy—relaxing," Stephanie replied. "Besides, Darcy's going to coach Allie and me. She's convinced she can make us into really good swimmers."

"Well, good for her," Danny said. "It's great to have a goal."

"Dad, it's only for fun," Stephanie told him. "I mean, it's not like we're training for the Olympics or something."

"Still, I think it's a great idea," Danny said.

"It sure is." Jesse glanced at the twins, who were climbing down from the table. "I hope the twins have lots of swimming at their day care center."

"They will, honey," Becky told him. "I made sure of that when I signed them up. In fact, all the parents I talked to there think their kids will have a terrific time. And that means the parents can relax, too."

"But I want to go swimming right now," Alex said. He grabbed Stephanie around the knees. "Take me with you, Stephie!"

"Take me, too," Nicky said.

"I can't," Stephanie told them. "For one thing, you guys won't fit on my bike."

"We don't care! Take us anyway," Alex said.

Jesse lifted Alex away from Stephanie. "Maybe we'll meet Stephanie at the pool later," he said. Jesse laughed when he saw the look of horror on Stephanie's face. "Don't worry, Steph," he added. "Only kidding. Promise."

Stephanie sighed in relief. "Thanks, Uncle Jesse. No offense, but the pool is sort of *my* special place for the summer." She gulped down the rest of her breakfast, then grabbed her backpack. "I'm late to meet Allie. Bye, everyone!" she called as she hurried out the door.

"Allie! Over here!" Stephanie waved wildly as she turned the corner onto Allie's block. Allie was standing on the sidewalk with her bike, scanning the street.

"You're late," Allie said as Stephanie glided up next to her.

"Sorry," Stephanie said. "I had a narrow escape at home. The twins wanted to come to the pool with me."

"You're kidding!" Allie exclaimed.

"It's okay," Stephanie told her. "They're going to day care instead. Michelle will be at the YMCA pool. And the rest of my family are too busy working to come by. They can only go on weekends."

"Good. Because having your family around would not be the best start to our big summer," Allie said.

"Tell me about it!" Stephanie laughed. She stepped away from her bike to show Allie her outfit. "So? What do you think? Do I look like someone who's cool enough to hang out at the pool on her own?"

Allie glanced at Stephanie and shuddered. "You look great, Steph," she said. "But your bike doesn't do much for your image."

Stephanie's bike was a hand-me-down from D.J. Its pink-and-purple paint was battered and scratched, and scraps of cartoon stickers still clung to the handlebars.

Stephanie frowned. "I didn't realize how babyish this bike looks. I guess I need a better one to fit my new, super-cool image. A new one, like yours," she said.

15

"That's one good thing about being an only child," Allie told her. "I get a new bike whenever I need it."

"Not me," Stephanie said. "If I asked for a new bike, my dad would probably tell me to go earn the money myself."

Stephanie swung back onto her bike, and they headed for the pool, riding side by side down the street.

"It would be tough to earn that much money," Allie told her.

"I know. I actually thought about it," Stephanie said. "D.J.'s working this summer to earn money for college. She found a great job in an office downtown."

"But she's older than us," Allie pointed out. "All we can do is baby-sit or something. Besides, having a job would mean that you couldn't hang out at the pool," Allie added. "And we've been looking forward to *that* for months."

"True. And I really do want to work on the cool, new me this summer," Stephanie said.

Allie hesitated. "You know, I made a sort of special promise to myself about that," she said.

"What kind of promise?" Stephanie asked.

"Well, I want to try to change this summer. I want to stop being so shy with boys," Allie said.

"Do you think I could do it? Could I learn to be more outgoing, like you and Darcy?"

"Absolutely!" Stephanie exclaimed. "Really, Al, you're so terrific. All you have to do is let a guy know you're interested in him. And then let him get to know you."

"I don't know if I could ever do that," Allie said.

"Sure you could," Stephanie told her. "After all, you have me and Darcy to help!" She grinned. "I say the boys at the pool better watch out. They're about to meet the three coolest girls ever!"

No doubt about it, Stephanie thought. *This summer will be our best summer yet!*

CHAPTER
3

◆ ◂ ◾ ◆

They reached the entrance to the community center. Stephanie and Allie locked their bikes in the bike rack. They showed their passes to the girl at the front gate, and she waved them inside.

"Darcy said to meet her by the clubhouse," Stephanie said.

The community center had several buildings scattered across its huge green lawn. The clubhouse and pool were right in the middle. The clubhouse contained the locker rooms, the snack shack, and offices. Beyond the clubhouse, a grove of trees shaded a dozen picnic tables. Nearby was a playground. Beyond that lay playing fields and a couple of volleyball courts.

Thick hedges blocked out the noise of passing traffic. It was hard to believe that the city of San Francisco was right outside the gates.

"There's Darcy," Allie said. Stephanie glanced up and saw Darcy jogging toward them from the clubhouse. She looked great in her light green swimsuit with a towel flung over one shoulder.

"Hey, you guys! Let's hit the water," Darcy said. "I want to see how fast I can get you in shape."

Darcy followed Stephanie and Allie into the locker room. She waited while they stashed their things and changed into their bathing suits. By the time they headed toward the pool, it was already crowded.

"Okay, time for a serious decision," Stephanie said. "We need to figure out the perfect spot to sit. We need just enough sun and just enough shade."

"How about here?" Darcy asked. "This spot *is* perfect—for checking out the action. Like the cute lifeguards!"

Stephanie glanced at the lifeguard chair at the head of the pool. A tall blond boy sat there. He wore a white tank top and red lifeguard shorts. A silver whistle hung around his neck. A red lifeguard's cap shaded his eyes. Another lifeguard with dark hair stood next to the chair, chatting with him.

"The blond guy is Rick, and the dark-haired guy

is Chad. They're both sixteen and assistant life-guards," Darcy said. "I heard some girls talking about them in the locker room," she added.

"They are totally cute," Allie said. "Especially Chad."

"Really? I think Rick is much cuter," Stephanie said. She couldn't help staring at the way the light gleamed on Rick's blond curls. *He really* is *amazing looking,* she thought.

"Donny!" a mother suddenly screamed across the pool. Stephanie turned to see what was the matter.

"Look!" Allie exclaimed, pointing at the low diving board. A little boy about three years old teetered on the edge of the board. He looked as if he would fall into the water at any moment.

Stephanie gasped. "Oh, no! How did he get there?"

"Donny! Don't jump!" his mother pleaded as she ran toward the diving board. "You can't swim!" she yelled.

As Stephanie watched, Rick sprang out of the lifeguard chair and raced toward Donny. Donny leaped off the diving board at the same instant. Rick dove into the water. Stephanie felt a nervous flutter in her stomach.

"Oh, Steph, what if that little boy drowns?" Allie asked.

"I know," Stephanie replied. "Little kids have no idea how dangerous the water can be." She thought of Alex or Nicky, and how scared she would be if one of them was in trouble.

Then Rick popped out of the water—with Donny in his arms. Rick was smiling as he spoke to Donny, pretending that nothing serious had happened.

"You're okay, big guy," he said. "But from now on, you're not allowed on the diving boards. Any of them! All right?"

"All right," Donny replied with a happy smile.

Donny's mother reached to take Donny from Rick. She wrapped her arms tightly around her little boy. "Oh, Donny—don't you ever do that again!" she scolded. She flashed Rick a grateful smile before carrying Donny away.

"Wow! I was so scared!" Allie exclaimed. "I thought that little kid would drown for sure!"

"Yeah. Rick was totally cool," Darcy said. "He hit the water almost before Donny did. He is one great lifeguard."

Stephanie stared at Rick as he toweled off and climbed back into the lifeguard chair. He acted as if nothing at all had happened.

"He was incredible," Stephanie muttered. She sighed. "He can rescue me anytime."

Allie glanced at her and giggled. "Uh-oh!" she teased. "Someone has a crush."

Stephanie colored. "I do not," she said.

"It's okay," Allie told her. "Rick *was* great." She paused. "But I still like Chad better."

"Now *you* sound like the one with a crush," Darcy said.

"Yeah. And you should put your money where your mouth is—and find a way to meet Chad," Stephanie added. "Remember what you said about boys?"

"Oh, sure, no problem," Allie replied with a nervous laugh.

"What's all this?" Darcy demanded. "What did Allie say about boys?"

Allie looked embarrassed. "Nothing! Just that I want to be less shy around them this summer," she explained.

"That's great!" Darcy told her. "Then you *should* go talk to Chad."

"How?" Allie asked. "What would I say?"

"Well, you could talk about Rick's big rescue," Darcy said.

"That might make Chad feel bad that *he* didn't rescue Donny," Allie pointed out.

"Oh." Darcy shrugged. "Well, I don't know, then. I guess you could ask him where the pay phone is."

"That is so lame!" Allie shook her head. "I'm not doing anything dumb like that," she said.

"You could always try drowning," Stephanie joked. "You jump in like Donny did and pretend to be drowning, and Chad dives in and rescues you. It's very romantic."

"Stop, you guys," Allie told them. "Really. I have all summer to work on the new me. I don't have to start right this minute."

"You're right, Al," Stephanie said. "But I'm going to start on my new, cool image right away."

"How are you going to do that?" Allie asked.

At that moment, Rick left the lifeguard chair and walked around the edge of the pool.

Stephanie stood up and smoothed her blue one-piece suit. "I'm going to meet Rick. I'll dive into the pool and then ask him for pointers on diving."

"Good luck," Darcy told her.

Stephanie stood and strolled toward the edge of the pool. She stopped a few steps away from Rick.

You're a good diver. You can do this! she told herself. *Just don't panic.*

Stephanie took a deep breath. She tensed her muscles and took a few running steps, getting ready to plunge gracefully into the water.

Tweeeeeeet!

A whistle blew loudly, right behind her. "No running at the pool!" a voice yelled.

Stephanie froze.

She'd know that voice anywhere. But it *couldn't* be!

Stephanie glanced over her shoulder. Rene Salter stood behind her, wearing a red lifeguard's tank suit. A silver whistle hung around her neck and a red cap sat on her head.

Stephanie stared at Rene in shock. "I don't believe this!" she exclaimed.

"Believe it," Rene replied.

"But what are you *doing* here?" Stephanie demanded.

"I'm an assistant lifeguard this year. Didn't you know?" Rene asked.

"That's impossible," Stephanie told her. "All the Flamingoes belong to the country club."

"The country club is closed for the summer. It's being fixed up," Rene told her. "Alyssa's an assistant lifeguard here, too. And our friends are coming to hang out with us. So I guess you and I will be together all summer long."

"Great," Stephanie muttered.

"Oh, it'll be lots of fun," Rene said. "All you have to do is obey the rules."

"And I know you'll love making me do that," Stephanie replied. "Well, there's no rule against jumping in the pool, is there?" Without waiting for an answer, Stephanie whirled around—and knocked right into Rick!

Rick lost his balance and toppled over the edge of the pool.

Splaaash!

He tumbled into the water.

"Oh, no!" Stephanie gasped in horror as Rick went under. His red lifeguard hat floated to the surface of the pool.

Rene's mouth dropped open in astonishment. "Good going, Stephanie!" she cried. "You just tried to drown the lifeguard!"

Stephanie stood frozen in embarrassment.

Rick swam up to the surface of the water. He spluttered as he reached blindly for the side of the pool. He looked as embarrassed as Stephanie.

Rene ran to the side of the pool and knelt down. "Rick! Are you okay?" she asked.

"Let me help you," Stephanie said. She knelt beside Rene and held out her hand to Rick. Rick grasped it tightly. For an instant, his deep blue eyes gazed straight into hers. Stephanie felt a jolt go through her.

Then Rick hoisted himself onto the edge of the pool and stood up. Rene immediately stepped between him and Stephanie. "I can't believe Stephanie did that! Are you really okay?" she asked.

"Yeah. Sure I am," Rick said. He shook the water

from his hair. "I was going to wash my hair today, anyway." He grinned.

"I'm so sorry," Stephanie added. She noticed Rick's hat still floating in the water. She leaned forward and fished it out of the pool. "Here's your hat," she said.

Rene snatched the hat away. She glared at Stephanie, then turned to Rick and held out the hat to him. She opened her blue eyes extra wide and gave him her sweetest smile. "Here, Rick," she said. "I hope it's not ruined."

Alyssa Norman ran up, dressed in her red lifeguard suit. She handed Rick a towel. "I can't believe Stephanie knocked you into the pool," she said. "That is so like her! She's a major klutz."

"Hey! I am not!" Stephanie protested.

Rick squinted at her. "So, I'm dealing with a dangerous klutz, huh?" he teased. "Do you go around pushing people every chance you get?" he asked.

"No, of course not!" Stephanie said. "I only push them every *other* chance."

Rick burst out laughing. "Good one," he said. He smiled at her.

I think he likes me! Stephanie thought.

"Excuse me, Rick," Rene said loudly. "Alyssa and I really need to go over some lifeguard stuff with you. Do you have a minute?"

26

"Uh, sure. Lifeguard business always comes first," Rick told her.

"Great. Let's go over to my chair," Rene said.

"Okay. See you," Rick said to Stephanie.

Rene placed a hand on Rick's arm as she led him away. "I bet you could use something cold to drink. Soda? Sparkling water? The Flamingoes have everything. And after all—you deserve the best." She flashed him another one of her biggest smiles—sweet and flirting and helpless.

Oh, no, Stephanie thought. *I recognize that look!*

It was the same look Rene used to give Kyle. It was the look Rene gave a boy when she really liked him.

Rene liked Rick!

And Stephanie liked him, too.

Stephanie groaned in dismay. *This can't be happening again!* she thought.

CHAPTER

4

◆ ◄ ▪ ◆

Stephanie hurried back to her pool chair.

"Stephanie, what is going on? What are Rene and Alyssa doing here?" Darcy asked.

"They're assistant lifeguards," Stephanie said. She explained what Rene told her.

"That's the end of our summer," Allie said. "We can't hang out with the Flamingoes here."

"That's not true," Darcy replied. "I mean, Stephanie wanted to meet Rick—and she *did* meet him, Rene or no Rene." Darcy chuckled. "Of course, knocking him into the pool was a strange way to do it, but it worked."

"And I saw the way Rick smiled at you, Steph," Allie added. "I think he's interested! And that's great!"

"Yeah, great," Stephanie replied. "Except for one problem. I think Rene likes Rick, too."

Allie's mouth dropped open. "You don't mean . . ."

"Yup. Rene and I like the same boy—again," Stephanie said.

Darcy groaned. "Which means that Rene will make your life totally miserable." She shook her head in pity. "Poor Stephanie."

"At least Rene and Alyssa are only assistant lifeguards," Allie said. "They're not the real big shots around here."

"Tell that to Rene," Darcy replied. "And her friends." She pointed across the pool.

Stephanie turned to look. The Flamingoes had arrived! Cynthia and Tiffany were trying to put up a pink umbrella decorated with pictures of tiny pink flamingoes. Bright pink fringe hung from the bottom.

Dominique, Darah, and Tina ran out of the clubhouse and joined them. They all wore matching pink bikinis. Loud squeals rang out as they pushed at the umbrella, which kept falling over. Rick and some other boys rushed to help. They lifted the umbrella into place and then arranged the girls' lounge chairs in a circle.

"Would you look at that?" Allie said. "Nobody helped us arrange our chairs!"

Stephanie watched with a sinking feeling in her stomach. Rick was the cutest, most amazing guy she had ever met. She liked him, and she thought he liked her. But how could anything ever happen between them with Rene and the Flamingoes hanging around?

Darcy was right. Rene would ruin everything. She was already laughing and smiling at Rick with her big, phony smile.

Rick headed back to the lifeguard chair. Stephanie was about to turn her head in relief when she saw a girl walking toward the Flamingoes. The girl was tall and slim. Her long blond hair blew across her face as she bent over a huge duffel bag while she walked. She was so busy checking inside her bag that she wasn't looking where she was going. She didn't see two boys walking right toward her. The boys were carrying trays of drinks from the snack shack.

"Hey, watch out for . . ." Stephanie began to yell.

Then everything seemed to happen in slow motion. The girl glanced up and saw the boys in front of her. She jumped in alarm and her bag swung out and knocked into one of the trays.

Drinks flew through the air. One large pink Slurpee headed right for Rene. She shrieked and leaped out of her chair as the Slurpee spilled all over her. Pink, sticky liquid dripped down the front of her red bathing suit.

Stephanie gasped.

"Are you crazy?" Rene screamed at the blond girl. "Why don't you look where you're going?"

The girl gaped at Rene. Her mouth opened, but no sound came out.

"Hey, that's Kayla Norris!" Darcy exclaimed. "She's a seventh-grader. She plays field hockey for St. Agnes. I met her at a tournament last year. She's a good athlete, though she's sort of the nervous type."

"She has a reason to be nervous now," Stephanie said. "Rene will kill her for dumping that Slurpee on her."

"Poor Kayla," Allie said. "I feel sorry for her already!"

"At least the Slurpee was pink," Stephanie said with a grin.

"Are you stupid or what?" Rene continued to yell at Kayla. "You wrecked my lifeguard suit!" Rene turned and glared at the other Flamingoes. "Somebody get this disgusting stuff off me!"

Alyssa and Cynthia leaped for their pink towels and began wiping off Rene's hair and tank suit.

"I'm s-s-sorry," Kayla finally stammered. She pulled a crumpled towel from her duffel bag and tried to hand it to Rene. As she stepped forward, she stomped on Rene's toe.

"Yeow!" Rene pushed Kayla. "Get away from me!" she shrieked.

"I've never seen Rene so mad!" Darcy said. She chuckled. "Someone should give Kayla a medal."

Stephanie jumped up from her chair. "Actually, someone should rescue her. She could probably use a friend right now."

Stephanie hurried across the pool. She saw Cynthia sneer at Kayla. "What are you standing there for?" Cynthia asked Kayla. "Don't you have someplace to go? Don't you have friends to sit with?"

"Of course she has friends," Stephanie said as she reached Kayla and Rene.

"I knew it!" Rene shrieked. "I knew you had something to do with this, Stephanie!"

"As if I made her trip and spill that drink on you!" Stephanie laughed.

"For all I know, you paid her to do it," Rene snapped. "Just get your little friend away from me."

"Come on, Kayla," Stephanie said. She pulled her toward their side of the pool. "You better come sit with us."

"Uh, who *are* you?" Kayla asked.

"My name's Stephanie, and I'm the person Rene

loved to hate—until you came along," Stephanie teased. "Welcome to the club."

Kayla turned pink. "I am a real klutz sometimes, it's true," she said.

"Yeah, but I hear you're also a great athlete," Stephanie told her. "And don't worry about being a klutz. I just knocked a lifeguard into the pool," she said.

Kayla laughed. "No! I bet you nearly died of embarrassment," she said.

"It's worse than that," Stephanie replied. She lowered her voice. "Rene hated me all last year because she liked this boy, but he asked *me* out."

"That's bad news," Kayla said.

"It gets worse," Stephanie told her. She nodded toward Rick. "See that lifeguard?"

"The blond one? He's really cute," Kayla said. "Is he the one you knocked in the pool?"

"Yeah," Stephanie said. "And I think he might like me. But there's a problem." Stephanie paused.

"Don't tell me," Kayla cut in. "Rene likes him, too."

Stephanie's mouth opened in surprise. "How did you guess?"

Kayla shrugged. "Well, Rene does seems to hate you," she said. "And liking the same boy as Rene is about the worst thing I can think of."

33

"You sound like you know Rene already," Stephanie said.

They reached Allie and Darcy. Stephanie dragged over an extra chair for Kayla, and everyone introduced themselves.

"Listen, don't worry about what happened with Rene," Darcy told her. "Those Flamingoes live to hate people."

"Wait—who are the Flamingoes?" Kayla asked, looking confused.

"They're a snobby club at our school. And Rene is their unofficial leader," Stephanie explained.

"Oh, no! And I just ruined her bathing suit!" Kayla groaned. "Sometimes I think making mistakes is my biggest talent," she said.

"Hanging out with us is no mistake," Stephanie told Kayla. "We're glad to have a new friend."

"Thanks. Because now that Rene is mad at me, I have a feeling I'll need all the friends I can get," Kayla said.

"Don't worry," Allie told her. "We'll protect you. Just stick with us for the rest of the summer."

"You're one of us now," Stephanie added. "The four of us can stick together. And then those Flamingoes better watch out!"

CHAPTER
5

♦ ◄ ► ♦

Stephanie glanced up as Allie steered her bike into the community center the next morning. Allie leaped off her bike and locked it in the rack. She had ridden over by herself that morning.

"Allie! What happened to your hair!" Stephanie exclaimed in shock. "It's red!"

"I know. Do you like it?" Allie asked, patting her head nervously. Her usual brown color had been replaced by tints of coppery red. "It's just a rinse," Allie explained. "I can wash it out again if you don't like it."

"But I love it!" Stephanie exclaimed. "It's perfect for the new you." She grinned. "And I bet Chad will love it, too."

Allie's eyes lit up. "Do you really think so?" she asked.

"Sure," Stephanie said. "I can't wait for him to see it."

They showed their passes at the gate and hurried into the pool area. Darcy raced up to them. She was wearing a big purple shirt over her bathing suit. "Hurry, you guys," she called. "Kayla and I saved chairs for us! Kayla's guarding them, but it's getting pretty crowded in there. She might need help." Darcy paused and squinted at Allie. "Hey. You rinsed your hair! It looks great," she said.

"Thanks," Allie replied. "I was afraid it was too red."

"No way!" Darcy exclaimed. "But hurry—we have to get those chairs."

Darcy led the way into the pool. She was right. The pool *was* crowded. There were already twice as many kids gathered around as yesterday.

Kayla rushed up to them, out of breath. "I'm sorry," she blurted. "I tried, but they took them away!"

"Whoa," Darcy said. "Who did what?"

"The Flamingoes! They took our chairs away," Kayla answered. "I tried to stop them. But they acted like I wasn't even there. Rene said they get first choice because they're lifeguards!"

Darcy shook her head. "I hate those Flamingoes," she muttered.

"I'm sorry. I should have done something," Kayla said.

"What could one of *you* do against all of *them?*" Allie asked.

"I guess." Kayla shrugged, then glanced at Allie again. "Hey—nice hair," she said.

Stephanie glanced across the pool. The Flamingoes had already set up their pink umbrella. A bunch of the older boys were arranging their chairs for them at the edge of the pool.

Rene, Alyssa, Tiffany, and a few others were busy spreading their pink towels over the chairs. A couple of little kids were racing back and forth to the snack shack, bringing them snacks to eat.

"Oh, who cares about those dumb Flamingoes, anyway? Let's just ignore them," Allie said.

Stephanie shook her head. "We can't," she replied. "If we let Rene get away with this, she'll just pull an even nastier trick the next time. We have to get those chairs back."

Kayla grinned. "I could spill drinks on them. That would make them get up in a hurry." She and Allie giggled.

"No—we should lift up the ends of their chairs and slide them right into the water!" Darcy said.

"I wish we were strong enough to do it," Stephanie told her. "Come on, guys, let's just go over there. We'll think of something."

Stephanie led the way to the Flamingoes' side of the pool. There were six girls seated around Rene. Rene glanced up as Stephanie stood over her. She and her friends exchanged amused looks.

"Oh, hi, Stephanie. Is something wrong?" Rene asked.

"You know it is. Those were our chairs," Stephanie said.

Rene raised an eyebrow. "Really? I didn't know these were special, private chairs," she said.

"I thought they belonged to the pool club," Tiffany added.

"Yeah, we didn't see your name on them anywhere," Cynthia said.

"You know what I mean," Stephanie replied. "Kayla was saving those four chairs for us."

"Alyssa and I are lifeguards," Rene said smoothly. "We get first choice of everything around here."

Stephanie frowned. "There's no rule like that," she replied. "Besides, you're only *assistant* lifeguards."

Rene scowled. She turned and nodded toward the lifeguard chair. Chad was on duty with a boy Stephanie didn't know.

"Why don't you go ask Chad and Mike what

they think?" Rene dared Stephanie. "But don't push them in the pool," she added.

Alyssa, Tiffany, and the other Flamingoes burst out laughing.

Stephanie felt her face flame red. But she tried to act calm. "All right, Rene," she said. "I *will* ask them!"

She stomped off toward the lifeguards. Allie, Darcy, and Kayla followed her. Chad and Mike stopped talking as they came near. Darcy nudged her forward. "Do it," Darcy whispered.

"Uh, hi," Stephanie said to Chad. "This is sort of embarrassing, but, well, the Flamingoes took our chairs."

"You mean, Rene and her friends?" Chad asked.

"Right," Stephanie said. "And, well, we need chairs."

"What we really need is something to scare those birds away," Allie muttered.

"You're right, Allie," Darcy said. "That is what we need, but we'll take chairs instead."

"I don't know why they need chairs," Chad replied. "I thought flamingoes stand in the water— on their long, bony legs." He laughed at his own joke.

Allie blinked at him in surprise. Chad grinned at her. "Hey—if you're an Allie, you already have something to scare them with," Chad went on. "An alligator. Allie's gator! Get it?"

Allie's mouth dropped open. She stared at Chad, and he grinned back at her.

Mike groaned. "Your puns are *so* bad!" he told Chad.

"Yeah, but you love them," Chad shot back. He grinned at Allie again, and this time Allie gave him a shy smile.

"Well, uh, seriously," Stephanie said to Mike. "The thing is, we really do need chairs, and Rene said that assistant lifeguards get first pick. That isn't true, is it?"

Mike looked at her as if she were crazy. "Who cares about some dumb chairs?" he asked. "There are plenty of places to sit." He pointed at the empty lawn surrounding the pool.

"There? You want us to sit there?" Stephanie asked. Families usually sat under the trees. It was definitely uncool.

"Why not?" Mike shrugged. "It's a nice, safe place. You know, far enough away that you can't knock any more lifeguards into the pool." He grinned.

Stephanie felt her face flush.

"Come on, Steph," Darcy said. "We can take a hint." She grabbed Stephanie's arm and marched to an empty spot under a big shade tree. Kayla followed them. "This spot isn't too bad," she said. "At least there aren't any families around."

"Or lifeguards," Stephanie muttered. "Did you hear what Mike said? I'm the joke of the pool! They're never going to let me forget what happened yesterday."

"Can you blame them? Lifeguards don't get knocked into the pool every day," Darcy teased. She and Kayla spread their towels over the grass.

Stephanie groaned as she spread out her own towel. "I'll never make it through this summer," she said.

Allie hurried up to them.

"Here's Allie. At least her summer is going right," Kayla said. "Did you talk more to Chad?" she asked.

"Not really," Allie admitted. "I said, 'Well, bye,' and then he said, 'See you.' " She dropped her head into her hands. "I can't believe I couldn't think of anything better to say!"

"You're lucky Chad picked you to talk to," Kayla said. "He's really cute. And he obviously likes you."

"Kayla's right. You *are* lucky," Stephanie added. "I mean, you decided to be different around boys, and you're already doing great with Chad."

"Just go back and talk to him more," Kayla told her.

"I can't," Allie said. She blushed scarlet. "I really can't! Help me, you guys. What should I say next?"

"Why don't you ask him to help with your swimming," Kayla suggested.

"But don't ask him right now," Stephanie said. "Because the Flamingoes are getting in the water."

Across the pool, Cynthia and Tiffany dove into the water. Rene climbed up on the lifeguard chair while Mike took a walk to patrol the pool.

"You're right. I'm not letting Rene see how badly I swim," Allie said. "We can swim later."

"Too bad more of our other friends don't come here," Darcy said. "Then we could take over the pool. Do you have friends who hang out here?" she asked Kayla.

"No," Kayla told her. "Nobody from St. Agnes swims here."

"I still can't believe you go there," Darcy said. "You guys know St. Agnes, right?" she asked. "It's that place with the horrible plaid uniforms."

"Darcy!" Allie said. "Shhh!"

"Kayla knows they're ugly," Darcy said with a grin. "Red-and-brown plaid doesn't look good on anyone."

"Very true," Kayla said. "They're totally disgusting. But at least I don't have to spend my allowance on school clothes."

"Speaking of clothes, I'd love some new summer outfits," Darcy said. "But I'm totally broke."

"Me too. Though I want money to buy a new bike," Stephanie said.

"I wouldn't mind earning money this summer, either," Kayla agreed. "But there are hardly any jobs we can do."

"And if we had jobs, we couldn't hang out at the pool and have fun," Allie added.

"I know." Darcy sighed. "Hey, look—the Flamingoes are getting out of the pool," she said. "And Rene's not in the lifeguard chair anymore."

"Great! Now's our chance," Stephanie said. "Let's hit the water. Darcy, you can show us some new strokes."

They all stood up. "Look at the Flamingoes now," Kayla said as they got closer to the pool. "They're giving themselves manicures! What a dumb thing to do at the pool."

"At least we're not wasting our time painting our toenails pink," Allie replied.

Stephanie heard a yell. "Watch it, you little brat!" Alyssa screeched.

Stephanie chuckled. Some little boys were playing with squirt guns, and they had accidentally squirted the Flamingoes.

Cynthia leaped off her chair. "Cut that out!" she screamed. "Go play somewhere else!"

"We can play here if we want to," one of the boys yelled back.

Rene came running up, blowing her whistle. "No water guns near the pool," she shouted.

"Who says?" one little boy asked.

"I say—so beat it!" Rene leaped at the boy, and he ran off with his friends.

"Rene sure has a great way with kids," Allie murmured.

"They like her about as much as we do," Stephanie agreed.

"She'd never win the baby-sitter of the year award, that's for sure," Darcy added. "She hasn't a clue how to handle little kids."

Kayla giggled. "I bet the Flamingoes never baby-sat in their lives," she said. "At least that's one thing I'm good at."

"Me too," Stephanie said. "I've sat for my little sister and my cousins so much that—" She suddenly stopped speaking. Her eyes lit up, and a slow grin spread across her face.

"Uh-oh," Darcy said. "I've seen that look before."

"Yeah—usually right before you get a great idea," Allie added. "And then we all get into trouble!"

"But not this time," Stephanie told her. "This is a *really* great idea. In fact, it's a truly amazing idea. And if it works, we'll have the perfect way to make money this summer—and have fun at the same time!"

CHAPTER
6

◆ ◀ ◗ ◆

"What's your amazing idea?" Darcy asked.

"A baby-sitting service—right here at the pool!" Stephanie's eyes sparkled.

"Are you serious?" Allie asked.

"Sure," Stephanie replied. "It's like my aunt Becky was saying yesterday—parents like to know that their kids are having fun in the summer. So we could offer to baby-sit for little kids right here at the pool. Then their moms and dads could have time to relax."

"And we could make a ton of money!" Darcy grinned. "It's a fantastic idea!"

"You're right," Allie said. "And we've all baby-sat before. So people could trust us."

"Not only that," Stephanie said, feeling more and more excited. "But we have a great connection here. Do you know Sandy Kovaks?" she asked.

"Isn't she the activities director at the pool?" Darcy asked.

"Right. She lives down the street from me," Stephanie told her. "I baby-sat her kids a couple of times last year. So she already knows I'm a good baby-sitter."

"That's fantastic!" Allie cried. "Do you think Sandy would let us sign people up for our baby-sitting service?"

"She might," Stephanie said.

"Then what are we waiting for?" Darcy asked. "Let's see Sandy right now."

The four girls hurried into the clubhouse. Sandy was just putting down the phone as they rushed into her office.

"Whoa, where's the fire?" Sandy asked. She grabbed at some papers that threatened to fly off her desk. She was a pleasant-looking young woman with short, reddish hair. She gave them a big, friendly smile.

"Sandy—I did a good job when I baby-sat your kids, didn't I?" Stephanie asked.

"You sure did. Why? Are you looking for more work?" Sandy asked.

"Yes, but not at your house," Stephanie said.

"My friends and I want to start a baby-sitting service right at the pool."

"We could work a few days a week," Darcy chimed in. "There are so many little kids running wild around here. Their parents could use some help taking care of them."

"That *is* an interesting idea," Sandy said. "You see, I always wanted to start a summer camp here. The community needs it, and it's a good way to show how much support the community center gets from the neighborhood." Sandy eyed them thoughtfully. "Do you think you could run a camp for little kids?"

Stephanie gazed at Sandy in surprise. "I don't know. What exactly would we have to do?"

"You could offer a program for several hours every day," Sandy replied. "And plan activities to keep the kids busy. It's really not so different from what you were suggesting."

"But we'd have to do it every day?" Darcy asked.

"Yes," Sandy said. "Parents need to count on you being here when they need you."

"We weren't thinking of working *every* day," Stephanie said.

"It is a big responsibility," Sandy said. "But you'll earn good money. And I'll be glad to help with the planning and supplies. And I'll also give you training in first aid and pool safety, though only the lifeguards can actually teach swimming."

Stephanie looked at Allie, Darcy, and Kayla. "What do you think, guys?"

"I guess we could give it a try," Kayla said. "I know I love working with little kids."

"Great," Sandy said. "I'll figure out how much to charge the parents. Then I think we should offer the first camp session for two weeks. That can be a trial period for you, to see if it will work or not. After the two weeks, we'll know if you can handle it."

"What if we can't?" Darcy asked.

"Then I'll have to find someone else to run the camp," Sandy said. "So what do you say?"

"It sounds good to me," Stephanie said.

Sandy glanced at the calendar on her desk. "Tomorrow is Saturday. Let's meet for an hour, first thing in the morning. Then you can start putting up posters and see how many people sign up."

"This is amazing," Stephanie said. "I can't wait to start!" She paused. "And, Sandy—don't worry about the trial period. Two weeks won't be hard at all. I know we can handle this!"

"Great. I'm glad you're so excited," Sandy replied. "I'll work out some more of the details tonight. And I'll see you all tomorrow morning."

Stephanie led the way out of Sandy's office. "Can you guys believe this?" she asked.

"A whole camp to ourselves," Darcy said, beaming. "It feels so important."

"It is important," Kayla said.

Allie frowned. "You *do* think we can handle this okay, don't you, guys?" she asked.

"It shouldn't be too hard—not if we all work together," Darcy added. "The four of us make an incredible team."

"Right," Stephanie agreed. "And don't forget, it's only a few hours a day for two short weeks. How hard could it possibly be?"

Stephanie held her marker above a blank sheet of poster board. "Okay—what do we call our camp?" she asked. It was early on Saturday morning. Stephanie, Darcy, Allie, and Kayla sat at a table in the picnic area of the community center. They were ready to organize their camp.

"How about the Community Pool Mini-camp?" Kayla suggested.

"Too boring," Darcy said. "We need something to make it sound exciting. Like Jungle Summer Adventure. Or Treasure Island Fun Camp or—"

"But we're not going on safari or finding buried treasure," Allie pointed out. "We have to list the real things we'll do."

"Good idea." Stephanie bent over the paper. "Let's see—we'll have games, snacks, arts and crafts . . ."

"What are you writing?" a voice asked. Two little girls about four years old peered over Stephanie's shoulder.

"It's about a camp we're starting," Stephanie said.

"Is it a club?" the black-haired girl asked. "We love clubs."

"Sure, clubs are great fun," Kayla said. "Don't you think so, Stephanie?"

"Oh, sure. And our club will be the best," Stephanie said.

"Can I join your club, Stephanie?" the redheaded girl asked.

"I want to join Club Stephanie, too," the black-haired girl said.

"Club Stephanie!" Darcy grinned. "That sounds cool."

"No, I don't want to name it after me," Stephanie protested.

"Why not?" Allie asked. "I think Club Stephanie is a great name."

"And the baby-sitting thing *was* your idea, Stephanie," Kayla pointed out.

"I agree. We *should* call it Club Stephanie," Darcy said.

"I want to join Club Stephanie," the redheaded girl repeated.

Darcy printed SIGN UP FOR CLUB STEPHANIE! across the top of a poster before Stephanie could protest. "Okay," she said to the little girls. "It's official. Why don't you both ask your moms if you can sign up for Club Stephanie today?"

"Okay!" The girls ran off.

"See? Instant hit," Allie said.

"Hi, Allie!" Chad strode up to the table. He was with a tall, skinny guy. They both wore red lifeguard shorts with white T-shirts. "Bring your gator today, Allie?" Chad teased.

"Oh! No, um, I guess I forgot," Allie said.

"This is Pete," Chad said, introducing his friend. "He's the senior lifeguard on duty with me today."

"Oh. Isn't Rick here?" Stephanie asked. She felt the others glance at her, and she blushed.

"No. He's not on this weekend," Chad told her.

Chad peeked at their flyers. "Sandy said you guys were starting a summer camp here. That's pretty cool," he told Allie.

Pete checked his watch. "Hey, Chad, we'd better go," he said.

"Okay. We'll catch you later," Chad said, looking straight at Allie.

"Sure," Allie answered. She dropped her eyes as Chad and Pete hurried away.

51

"Way to go, Allie!" Darcy cheered. "Chad *definitely* likes you."

"Yeah, but what am I going to do about it?" Allie asked. "You guys were supposed to help me think of things to say to him, but you never did."

"Well, now you can talk to him about our camp," Stephanie said. "Let's hurry and write up our flyer. We'll make copies and give them to everyone before we leave today."

About a half hour later, Sandy came by to give them their course in first aid and water safety. They learned mostly how to help the lifeguards, who were in charge of those things. Then they posted flyers at the clubhouse, the pool, the playing fields, and in the locker rooms. By the end of the morning, the community center was covered.

They were heading back to Sandy's office when someone tapped Stephanie on the shoulder. She whirled around and saw a dark-haired, freckle-faced girl.

"Excuse me. But are you Stephanie? As in Club Stephanie?" the girl asked.

Stephanie stared at her. "Uh, yeah, I'm Stephanie," she said.

"I'm Anna. Anna Rice," the girl said.

Anna had a wide, pretty face. Her hair was held in place by a headband made of braided leather. Bright beads were knotted into the headband.

Stephanie thought the headband was unusual—and pretty. But the rest of Anna's outfit was just plain weird.

Anna wore a long black skirt that looked as if it was made out of old pieces of fabric tied together. She wore the skirt with a bright tank top that was tie-dyed in about a million clashing colors. She wore piles of beaded necklaces over it. There were at least a dozen of them, and they didn't exactly go together.

She also wore a stack of odd bangle bracelets on each wrist. The bracelets had strange, lumpy beads on them.

"I am *so* glad I found you!" Anna exclaimed. "I saw your flyer! I already talked to Sandy about it—isn't she great? And I can't believe you had almost the same idea I had! Sandy and I both think this club thing will be terrific."

"Um, thanks," Stephanie said. She glanced at Allie, who raised her eyebrows and shrugged. "So can I help you find Sandy?" Stephanie asked Anna.

"No!" Anna laughed. "That's funny. I guess you don't get it at all. I don't need Sandy. Sandy said *I* could help *you!*"

Stephanie gave Anna a blank look. "Help me?" she asked.

"With arts and crafts," Anna explained. "I just moved into the neighborhood. I'll be transferring to John Muir next year, and I was looking for a way to meet kids my age this summer," Anna went on. "So it's a perfect match."

"I don't get it," Stephanie said. "What are you talking about?"

"Teaching arts and crafts for Club Stephanie!" Anna exclaimed. "It's perfect! I'll get to know you guys and help you out at the same time."

"Oh! Well . . ." Stephanie didn't know what to say. She glanced at the others for help.

"Well, see, it's true that none of us really knows much about arts and crafts," Allie began. "But you see—"

"We really wanted to work together, just the four of us," Darcy finished. She pointed to herself, Stephanie, Allie, and Kayla. "We're kind of a team."

"Oh." Anna's smile faded.

Stephanie suddenly felt awful. She hated to be mean. And they really *could* use help with arts and crafts.

"Listen, Anna. Maybe we could—" Stephanie started to say.

"Uh-oh—here comes trouble," Darcy interrupted, grabbing Stephanie's arm.

Stephanie glanced up to see Rene leaving the locker room. Alyssa, Cynthia, Dominique, and Tiffany clustered around her. Rene caught sight of Anna and stopped in her tracks.

"Oh, look at Stephanie's new friend!" Rene exclaimed in a loud, clear voice. "She must think it's Halloween—because she's already wearing her witch costume!"

Stephanie wanted to sink into the ground. She felt awful for Anna.

"No, it's not Halloween," Anna told Rene in a calm voice. "I wore these beads today because I want to teach arts and crafts. And these beads were made by sick kids in the hospital. I taught them how." She smiled at Rene. "You're not making fun of sick kids, are you?"

Rene's cheeks turned pink. "No. Of course not. Those beads are, um, very nice," she murmured.

Stephanie exchanged amused looks with Darcy, Allie, and Kayla. Anna really knew how to handle the Flamingoes!

Stephanie grinned. "I guess you haven't met Anna yet," she said to Rene. "But she's going to be our new arts and crafts counselor." Stephanie turned to her friends. "Right, guys?"

"Right," Allie, Darcy, and Kayla said together. Anna beamed at them.

Rene frowned. "I saw your dumb posters," she said. "Club Stephanie! What makes you think you can run a kids' camp, anyway?" she demanded.

"Well, Sandy asked us to do it, and we think it'll be great," Stephanie told them. "We'll have games and crafts and swimming, and—"

"Swimming?" Rene laughed. "Now I know you're going to bomb!"

"What are you talking about?" Stephanie asked.

Rene gazed calmly at Stephanie. "You need the lifeguards to help you with swimming. And you won't get any help from Rick. Not after what he said about you."

"What do you mean?" Stephanie demanded. "What did he say?"

CHAPTER
7

♦ ◄ ▸ ♦

Rene snickered at Stephanie. "I guess you think Rick likes little girls who flirt with lifeguards. You probably think pushing him in the pool was cute."

"What did Rick say about me?" Stephanie demanded. She took a step closer to Rene.

"Oh, it was nothing," Rene teased. "He only said that babies like you are barely old enough to be allowed at the pool on their own."

"Hey, listen, Rene," Darcy began. "You're only one year older than us, and—"

"Yes. But that one year makes a *big* difference— to a sixteen-year-old boy." Rene tossed her head. "Rick thinks you're a baby, Stephanie. And so do I," she added. She linked arms with Alyssa and began to walk away. The other Flamingoes followed them.

"You'll see," Rene said. She raised her voice so that Stephanie and the others could hear every word. "Club Stephanie can't possibly work. Not with a big baby running it. I bet she doesn't make it through her first week."

Rick didn't say that, Stephanie told herself. *He didn't!*

"Ignore her, Steph," Darcy said. "She knows Rick likes you, and she's just jealous."

"Yeah, and she's probably jealous of Club Stephanie, too," Allie added. "Rene knows *she's* too much of a baby to run a whole camp. Sandy would never trust her with little kids!"

"I guess," Stephanie said. "Anyway, it doesn't matter what Rene says. Camp starts Monday. Then we'll see who's a baby or not!"

"Allie!" Stephanie gasped. "There must be a hundred of them! How did this happen?"

Stephanie stared ahead of her in dismay. It was Monday morning, the first day of Club Stephanie. And the picnic area was filled with four-year-old kids. Squirming, squealing, noisy kids. A whole group of mothers was waiting with them for camp to begin.

"Sandy said a lot of parents signed up. But I

had no idea this many kids would actually be here today," Stephanie said. "How will we ever handle them all?"

"I don't know. But this is Club Stephanie, and you're Stephanie," Darcy said, giving her a shove. "So you go meet them first."

"Thanks a bunch," Stephanie said. She put on a big smile as she approached the waiting kids and their mothers. "Hi, everyone," she called over the noise of the children. "Welcome to Club Stephanie! I'm glad to see you all here. Before we get started, Anna and Darcy will give out name tags for everyone."

Anna and Darcy grabbed the felt animals they had cut out for name tags. Anna knelt down by a cute little four-year-old girl.

"Hi! What's your name?" Anna asked. "And what kind of animal do you want?"

"I'm Kelly. And I want the bunny!" Kelly said.

Anna wrote Kelly's name on a pink felt bunny and pinned it to her T-shirt.

Stephanie grinned at Allie. "See? We have everything under control." She clapped. "Okay, everybody," she called to the kids. "Find a place at a table. Camp is about to start."

The parents slipped away as the kids ran to grab seats. One little boy with blond curls refused to sit down. He ran from table to table, making airplane noises. His name tag read AUSTIN. Kayla grabbed his hand.

"Austin, I have a special seat for you—it's where airplane pilots sit," Kayla told him. She led Austin to an empty seat next to a boy named Tyler.

"Okay, listen up, everybody," Stephanie said. "My name is Stephanie. This is Allie, Darcy, Anna, and Kayla. Before we start having fun, we'd like to go over the rules with you."

She started reading from the list they had made yesterday morning. "This is our camp headquarters. No one leaves the picnic area alone. Always be kind to the other campers and treat them like—"

"Ow! Quit shoving me!" Tyler yelled at Austin.

"Austin, please be nice," Stephanie said.

"When are we going to do something?" Austin demanded. "I'm bored."

"I'm hungry," another kid added. "Is it snack time?"

"No, but it's time for our first fun activity," Anna quickly said. "Right, Stephanie? We'll read the rules *later*. Now, who can draw a great big picture of themselves?" she asked. Twenty-four hands waved in the air.

"I hate drawing. I want to play a game," Austin said. "Let's play football!"

"Later, Austin," Stephanie told him. She helped

Darcy and Anna hand out markers and crayons. Allie and Kayla gave out the paper. Soon all the kids were drawing. Austin drew a quick smiley face.

"I'm done!" Austin waved his paper at Stephanie.

"Me too," Tyler said. Soon all the kids were done drawing.

Stephanie glanced nervously at Anna. "What'll we do?" she whispered. "This activity was supposed to last fifteen minutes. It's only been five minutes!"

Anna frowned. "I guess I forgot that little kids can't do one thing for too long."

"I want to play roller hockey," a large boy named Frederick said.

"I don't know how!" Kelly seemed about to cry.

Stephanie exchanged uncomfortable looks with her friends. They had to come up with an activity that *all* the kids liked.

"Roller hockey isn't a good idea, Frederick," Stephanie told him. "We don't have the equipment for it, and some kids can't skate yet."

"Besides, we have to stay on the lawn for now," Kayla added. "And you can't skate on grass."

"Then what can we do?" Frederick demanded.

"Let's play dodgeball," a boy named Josh said.

"Good idea," Stephanie said. Sandy had given her several balls to play with. They divided the kids into two groups and had them form two circles. Josh and Frederick were in Stephanie's group. Josh threw the ball hard and hit a little girl named Janie. Janie burst into tears. Then Frederick grabbed the ball away and tried to start his own game. Janie stopped crying, but she plopped onto the grass and refused to move. Frederick and Josh started wrestling.

"Do something!" Allie begged Stephanie. "This is turning into a disaster!"

Stephanie helped Allie and Anna get the girls started on another arts and crafts project. Then she and Darcy rounded up the boys again and tried to begin a game of tag.

Suddenly Stephanie heard shouts from the playground. Austin and Tyler had slipped away from the group and were racing each other to the top of the jungle gym.

"Austin! Tyler!" Stephanie shouted as she rushed after them. "Get back here, you guys. Remember the rules? You're not allowed in the playground by yourselves!"

Tyler and Austin climbed down, and Stephanie herded them back to camp. Darcy motioned for Stephanie to meet her, Allie, Anna, and Kayla at an empty table.

"I don't want to scare you guys," Darcy said in a low voice. "But we've already gone through half our list of activities—and we still have an hour and a half of camp left to go!"

Allie swallowed hard. "I'm not sure what to do next," she said.

"Me either," Kayla said.

"When in doubt, eat," Stephanie whispered. She stood and clapped for attention. "Okay, snack time," she yelled.

The kids dropped what they were doing and started running toward Stephanie.

Allie glanced at the carton filled with snacks for the day. "Hey, you guys—I don't think we have enough to go around. We only have enough to give them one slice of apple and one graham cracker each."

Stephanie sighed. "If we're lucky, some kids won't want anything to eat."

They quickly divided the food among the different tables. Then Stephanie met with Allie and the others. "They're almost done eating. So what do we do next?" she asked, feeling desperate.

"We could take them swimming," Darcy said.

"But we're not supposed to use the pool for another half hour," Kayla pointed out.

"We have to. This is an emergency," Stephanie told her. As the kids finished eating, she and the others helped them take off the shorts and T-shirts they wore over their bathing suits. They divided the kids into two lines and marched them toward the pool.

As they crossed the picnic area, Stephanie spotted another group of little kids gathered around a table. Squeals and giggles rang through the air.

"I wonder what's happening over there," Kayla said.

"I'll go see!" Austin yelled. He took off running before anyone could stop him.

"I'll get him," Stephanie said. She ran after Austin as he raced up to the table.

"Face painting! Cool!" Austin yelled. "Can I be a lion?"

Stephanie gasped. Several boys and girls were gathered at the table having their faces painted. And the Flamingoes were doing the painting!

Rene looked up as Stephanie approached her. "Hi, Stephanie. Would you like your face painted, too?" She giggled.

"Have a flyer," Cynthia told her. She handed Stephanie a colorful flyer. It looked as if it was created by a professional printer. Stephanie read through it quickly.

LITTLE FLAMINGOES DAY CAMP
FUN IN THE SUN!
* ARTS AND CRAFTS * DELICIOUS SNACKS *
SWIMMING LESSONS WITH TRAINED LIFEGUARDS

Stephanie felt as if she were about to explode. "Just what do you think you're doing?" she demanded. "You can't start your own camp."

"But Sandy gave us permission," Rene replied.

"Right," Alyssa added. "Your camp was filled up. But there are other kids around. Enough for two camps."

"But this camp was my idea. You stole my idea," Stephanie said in disbelief.

"No, we didn't. Rene was thinking of doing a camp, too, weren't you, Rene?" Alyssa asked.

"Absolutely," Rene answered.

"Sure—after you saw me doing it," Stephanie muttered under her breath.

"I guess you can't have everything you want," Rene snapped. She glared at Stephanie.

"Are you talking about camp?" Stephanie demanded. "Or about guys?"

"Listen, you—" Rene began.

Alyssa cut her off. "Don't argue about it," she said. "Sandy told us we should all work together."

"Oh, I'll believe that when I see it," Stephanie replied.

"Listen, Stephanie, we're going to have two camps, so get used to it!" Rene told her. "You'll have your camp, and we'll have ours." She glanced over Stephanie's shoulder and grinned. "Or maybe I should say, we'll also have *yours*."

65

Stephanie spun around. The Club Stephanie campers were racing toward the face-painting table. They swarmed around the table, yelling and laughing in excitement. "I want to be a kitten," Kelly shouted.

"Can you paint zombies?" Tyler asked.

Stephanie exchanged a helpless look with Darcy. "Sorry, Steph," Darcy said. "We couldn't hold them back. They love face painting."

Rene smirked. "You should really find something fun for your kids to do," she said. "Then they wouldn't want to leave Club Stephanie and join the Little Flamingoes."

Rene beamed at the little girl in front of her. "We're having so much fun, right, Angela?"

"Right," Angela replied.

Darcy pulled Stephanie away. "I don't believe this," she murmured.

"I do," Stephanie said. "Rene will do anything to get back at me!"

"And at our camp," Allie added.

"Yeah, but what are we going to do about it?" Kayla asked.

"I don't know. But I know one thing—we can't let the Flamingoes run a better camp than us," Stephanie said. "We have to prove that our camp is the best."

"And we have to show them they can't push us around," Kayla added.

"Right," Darcy agreed. "We're not afraid of Rene."

"No way," Stephanie agreed. "Rene's about to find out what kind of 'baby' she's dealing with. She's the one who should be afraid. Because this is war!"

CHAPTER
8

♦ ◀ ◆ ♦

Stephanie dumped an armful of supplies onto the picnic table. It was Tuesday morning, the second day of Club Stephanie. "Only fifteen minutes before our campers get here," she said.

"Great," Anna replied. "That should be plenty of time to set up our first activity."

"And time to talk to Sandy, too," Allie added.

"I don't want to talk to Sandy," Stephanie told her. "Not until our camp is running better."

"Sorry, Steph," Darcy said. "But you have no choice. Sandy is heading right this way."

Stephanie glanced up. Sandy was hurrying toward their table. "Hi, girls," she called. "Can I talk with you all for a minute?"

"Uh, sure," Stephanie answered.

Sandy sat on one of the picnic benches. Stephanie and Darcy took places next to her. Anna, Allie, and Kayla found seats on the other side.

"I understand you had some problems yesterday," Sandy began.

"Only some little first-day problems," Stephanie said.

"Really?" Sandy replied. "I heard that you couldn't control your campers. You know, girls, they have to be watched all the time. You can't let little kids run wild."

"They weren't running wild," Darcy told her.

"I heard they were in the jungle gym without any counselors," Sandy said.

"Well, uh, only for a few minutes," Stephanie said.

"A few minutes is too many," Sandy said. "I also heard they spent more time with Rene's group than with yours," Sandy went on. "Rene seemed very upset about it."

"Rene told you that?" Stephanie asked.

"Wow. That's not true!" Anna exclaimed. "I mean, our kids *did* go over to Rene's group, but only when she did face painting."

"And *we're* going to do face painting with our kids today," Kayla said.

"Right," Stephanie added. "In fact, we had a

special meeting yesterday when camp was over. We came up with great new ideas for our campers. We decided to divide them into smaller groups, say, four or five kids, with one counselor in charge of each group. Then we can work together or separately, depending on the activity."

"We spent yesterday afternoon brainstorming about how to make camp better today," Darcy said. "See all the supplies we brought?"

Darcy showed Sandy the stacks of things lined up on the picnic table. "We're going to frost cookies and make candy faces on them," she said.

"And we'll make friendship bracelets," Anna added.

"And have some fun relay races after snack time," Allie put in. "The kids will balance cotton balls on a spoon and push eggs with their noses across the ground."

"And we were careful to choose activities that both the boys and the girls would like," Stephanie told Sandy.

"It does sound like you're getting better organized," Sandy said.

"We are," Stephanie told her. "Really, Sandy, you can't listen to everything Rene says. She was only saying that stuff because she wants to get all the kids into *her* camp."

"I see," Sandy said slowly. "Well, I want you all

to understand something. I didn't expect your two camps to be rivals. There should be enough campers for two groups. Two groups that know how to cooperate," Sandy went on.

"But we—" Stephanie began.

"I told Rene I'd like your groups to plan some joint activities. Rene said she understood that," Sandy said.

Yeah, right, Stephanie thought. *As if Rene would ever cooperate with us!*

"Do you understand it, too?" Sandy asked.

"Of course!" Stephanie said. Allie, Darcy, Kayla, and Anna agreed.

Sandy frowned. "I like you girls," she said. "And I hope you straighten things out. But remember, you must have this camp running smoothly by the end of the trial period. If not . . ." Her voice trailed off.

If not, Rene will be glad to take over—and we'll never hear the end of it! Stephanie thought.

"Don't worry, Sandy," Stephanie told her. "We'll make this the best camp you ever saw. We're not going to give up—ever."

Sandy glanced at her watch. "All right, then. Your campers will be here in a minute," she said. "Better get ready."

"Good luck to us," Kayla muttered under her breath.

Sandy smiled. "I know little kids are a handful. But you're not alone. Come find me if you need extra help," she said. She stood up. "But make sure you don't take your eyes off them for a second, okay?" She gave the girls another smile and then hurried off again.

"Phew!" Darcy said. "For a moment, I thought we might lose the camp."

"Never," Stephanie said. "We'll never let that happen. We'll never let the Flamingoes win."

"I hate the way Rene went running to Sandy, trying to make trouble for us," Kayla said.

"She'd do anything to make us look bad," Darcy added angrily.

"Don't worry," Stephanie told them. "We'll just have to make sure that everything goes perfectly— starting now. Because here come the kids!"

Stephanie felt a nervous tingle as Austin, Kelly, and Josh rushed up to the table. About a dozen other kids followed. "Okay. What's first on our list?" she asked.

"Circle time and songs," Allie said.

Stephanie clapped for attention. Soon the kids were arranged in one big circle.

"I'm glad you know 'The Wheels on the Bus' and 'The Wiggling, Giggling Worm,'" Kayla whispered.

"I've heard the twins sing them a million times

at home," Stephanie replied. "If you'd heard that, you'd know them by heart, too."

All the kids knew the songs—and enjoyed shouting them out. Stephanie glanced at their happy faces.

This is just how I imagined camp would be! she thought. "Okay, guys. Now let's all be wiggling, giggling worms," she said.

"No way," Tyler said. "That's a little baby song. I'm a big boy."

Stephanie gulped. "Uh, well . . ."

"Well, sing it like a big boy, then," Kayla put in. Stephanie shot her a grateful smile. They began the song.

Josh made faces at Frederick. "Cut it out," Frederick said. He pushed Josh, and Josh pushed back. Suddenly the two boys were wrestling on the ground. The other kids jumped up to watch them. Some of the boys started cheering and yelling.

Stephanie and Kayla raced over to them and pulled them apart. "Okay, Frederick and Josh," Stephanie began. "Let's have a contest to see who—"

"Stephanie!"

Stephanie whirled around. Sandy was behind her, looking upset. "Are those your kids?" she asked. Stephanie looked where Sandy was pointing. Austin and Tyler were in the playground, climbing to the top of the jungle gym.

"Oh, no! Not again!" Stephanie muttered. She felt her face turn bright red.

"I told you to watch them more closely," Sandy said.

"We will!" Stephanie promised. "Take over here, Darcy. I'll go get them down," she added to Sandy.

Stephanie raced into the playground. Austin saw her coming and scrambled to the very top of the jungle gym.

"Austin, please come down," Stephanie said. "Uh, we're waiting for you to sing the next song."

"I'm busy right now," Austin said. "Tyler and I are flying a plane." He laughed.

Stephanie felt as if Sandy's eyes were staring a hole right through her. She lowered her voice. "Please, Austin," she said. "If you come down, I'll, um . . . let you choose the next song."

"Who cares?" Austin replied.

Stephanie bit her lip. *Sandy is going to fire me for sure,* she thought.

Kayla appeared beside Stephanie. "Tower to Austin. Tower to Austin!" she called through cupped hands. "Here are your landing instructions. Runway four is open. Time to land now."

"Aye, aye, tower!" Austin and Tyler swung

themselves down and dropped to the ground. They ran back to the circle, making airplane noises.

Stephanie sighed in relief. "Thanks again, Kayla," she whispered.

"No problem," Kayla whispered back. She and Stephanie hurried up to the circle of kids.

"Let's move on to face painting," Stephanie told them.

"Great! I want to be a werewolf," Frederick called.

"I want to be Dracula with blood dripping out of my mouth!" Tyler added.

"Okay," Stephanie said. "Line up. Everyone will get painted." She looked at Sandy. "Everything's fine now," she told her.

"Good," Sandy replied. "I'll check in with you later. Have fun!"

Sandy headed off to another area of the pool. Stephanie and Allie helped the kids line up in front of Anna, Darcy, and Kayla, who were doing the face painting.

"So far, so good," Stephanie muttered to Allie. "Running this camp is harder than I thought. It makes D.J.'s office job look easy!"

"How's that going?" Allie asked.

"Great." Stephanie giggled. "Though, I think she's jealous that I get to work in a bathing suit— and she has to wear a *business* suit!"

A loud cheer rang through the air. Stephanie swung her head at the sound. The campers turned to look, too.

Across the lawn, they saw a pink umbrella where Rene had set up camp. A huge banner hung from a nearby tree: LITTLE FLAMINGOES CAMP. ALL KIDS WELCOME!

"We're the Flamingoes, and no one could be prouder!" the Little Flamingoes chanted. "And if you don't believe us, we'll yell a little louder!"

"They're doing real cheers," Jennifer said. "With real pom-poms! I'm going over there!"

"Me too," Kelly said. "Cheers are more fun than dumb old face painting!"

Before Stephanie could stop them, Kelly and Jennifer ran over to the Flamingoes' camp. Lisa and Trisha followed them. Stephanie saw Rene, Alyssa, and Tiffany hand them all pink pom-poms.

"Kelly! Lisa! Come back!" Allie yelled.

But the girls kept running—and they didn't look back.

"Oh, no!" Stephanie exclaimed. "The Flamingoes are stealing our campers!"

CHAPTER
9

◆ ◀ ◆ ◆

"We won't have any girl campers left in a minute," Stephanie said. She turned to Darcy. "Do something—fast," she begged.

"Hey, everybody! It's pool time!" Darcy announced.

The kids all cheered. "Yay! We love swimming," Tyler cried.

Stephanie breathed a sigh of relief. "Thanks, Darce," she said. "That worked like a charm."

They hurried their campers down to the pool. Stephanie stopped short. "Oh, no," she whispered to Darcy. "Rick is on duty!" Her throat suddenly felt dry. Her palms felt sweaty.

"So what?" Darcy asked. She peered closely at

Stephanie. "You're not worried about what Rene said, are you? About Rick thinking you're a baby?"

"A little bit," Stephanie admitted.

Darcy laughed. "Oh, come on, Steph! She probably made that up! Rick likes you, I know it." She nudged Stephanie playfully in the ribs. "Just don't knock him down, and everything will be fine."

Stephanie gave Darcy a weak smile. "I'll try," she said. She took a deep breath to steady her nerves, then walked up to the pool at the head of the line of campers.

"Hey, wait a minute—you guys are here early, aren't you?" Rick called to her from the lifeguard chair. He checked his watch. "Don't you know how to tell time?" he teased.

"Of course I do!" Stephanie bristled. "I know we're early, but we—"

Oops! Calm down, Stephanie, she told herself. *He didn't say you were too babyish to tell time!*

Rick gave her a strange look, then shrugged. "I just meant I didn't expect your group yet," he said.

"Well, we have to swim now. Is that a problem?" Stephanie asked.

"Nope," Rick replied. "Just as long as you don't let any of your kids drown."

"Isn't that what you're here for?" Stephanie asked. "To save people?"

"Not me—I don't want to get my hat wet again," Rick joked. "It's already shrunk."

"Or else your head's getting bigger," Stephanie shot back.

Rick raised his eyebrows, as if he wasn't sure if they were joking or not.

Darcy poked Stephanie in the ribs. "Hey, lighten up," she muttered. "You don't have to take his head off."

"I know," Stephanie whispered back. "I didn't mean to—it just slipped out."

"Well, maybe you shouldn't talk to him for a while," Darcy said.

"Good idea." Stephanie nodded to Rick. "Uh, later," she said. She hurried after the kids. They whipped off their T-shirts and shorts and piled into the shallow end of the pool.

"Remember the rules," Stephanie called to them. "Stay in the shallow water—and keep near your pool partner at all times."

Darcy and Allie jumped into the pool with the kids. Kayla went to get balls and rings for the kids to play with. Anna and Stephanie watched the kids from the pool deck.

"Hey, Tyler, I'm a killer whale," Austin yelled. He went under and came up with a mouthful of water. He spat in Tyler's direction.

"I'm a whale, too," Tyler shouted. He started

spitting water, too. A little girl named Pam got an eyeful of water and started crying.

"Hey, no spitting water, Austin," Stephanie commanded. "We're going to play with water rings in a minute."

Kayla came back with the rings. She tossed them into the pool. "Okay, everyone," she said. "Grab a ring and pass it to your buddy."

"This is great," Stephanie said to Anna. "Even Austin should behave while we play this."

"Where is Austin?" Anna asked.

"He's right here," Stephanie said. She glanced at the water. "Wait—he *was* right here," she said.

"There he is!" Anna exclaimed. Austin was out of the pool, sneaking toward the clubhouse.

"Austin, come back here!" Stephanie yelled. Austin gave a quick glance over his shoulder. He started to run. Stephanie ran, too. She had almost reached him when he slid and fell on the concrete path.

"Austin! Are you okay?" Stephanie knelt by his side. One of his knees was lightly skinned. Austin looked at the tiny drops of blood and let out a wail.

"I'm bleeding!" he screamed.

"It's okay, Austin," Stephanie said in her most soothing voice. "You're fine. It's only a little scrape."

"It is not!" Austin yelled. He threw himself onto the ground, screaming. "You pushed me!"

"I did not," Stephanie said. Austin screamed even louder. Stephanie felt a burst of irritation.

"Cut it out, Austin," she snapped. "You're not really hurt, so stop crying!"

"Oh, real nice," a voice said. "That's a great way to comfort a little kid!"

Stephanie looked up. Rick was standing over her.

"He's not really hurt," Stephanie started to say. "He was running away and fell. He's a trouble-maker and—"

"A troublemaker? My little brother?" Rick glared at Stephanie.

Gulp! "Austin is your little brother?" Stephanie asked in a tiny voice.

Austin held out his arms to Rick. "Ricky, I hurted myself," he said.

Rick squatted down beside Austin. "You sure did, fella," he said. He turned to Stephanie with a puzzled expression on his face. "What's going on with you, anyway? Why are you picking on my brother?" he asked.

"I, uh, I—" Stephanie stuttered.

Rick helped Austin stand up. "It's okay, pal. We'll get you cleaned up, and you'll be as good as new."

Rene appeared holding a first aid kit. "I heard what happened!" she exclaimed. "What a terrible accident. Really, a counselor should be more responsible than this," she added, giving Stephanie a stern look.

"Come off it, Rene—I am responsible," Stephanie said.

"Right," Rene muttered. She bent over Austin. "You poor thing," she said in her sweetest voice. "Let me help clean you up. Okay, Austin?"

Austin gave Rene a shaky smile. "Okay," he said.

"Stephanie! What happened?" Stephanie looked up to find Sandy hurrying toward them. Alyssa was beside her.

"I brought Sandy like you told me to, Rene," Alyssa said with a smirk.

Naturally! Stephanie groaned.

"And I'm glad she did," Sandy replied. "You'd better explain this, Stephanie," she said. "I heard that you chased this little boy away."

"No! I mean, I had to," Stephanie said. "He was running away, and—"

"That's not how you handle a little kid," Rene told her.

Sandy stepped closer to Stephanie. "Look, Stephanie," she said in a low voice. "I understand that his behavior might be a problem. But now I have a problem. Some parents are asking if you and your friends are ready to run a camp."

"I'm sorry, Sandy," Stephanie said. "We're trying our best, really."

Sandy sighed. "I think we need to talk some more," she said. "I want to see all you Club Stephanie girls in my office—the moment camp is over today."

Rene smirked. "Come on, Austin," she said. "Let's go in the clubhouse with Sandy and get that knee cleaned up. Can you help us, Rick?"

Rick nodded. He took one of Austin's hands. Rene took the other. Sandy walked beside them as they headed toward the clubhouse. Stephanie watched, feeling miserable.

Allie raced up to Stephanie. "I saw everything," she said. "And it wasn't your fault, Steph."

"Don't tell me—tell Rick," Stephanie said. "Now he thinks I'm mean to his little brother."

Allie gasped. "Austin is Rick's brother?"

Stephanie nodded. "And that's not all. Sandy wants us to have a big meeting after camp." She swallowed hard. "I hate to say this, Allie. But right now, things don't look too good for Club Stephanie."

CHAPTER
10

◆ ◀ ◆ ◆

Stephanie closed the door to Sandy's office behind her. Their meeting lasted twenty long minutes, but now it was over.

"Well, that wasn't a *total* disaster," Darcy said.

"No. We got off pretty easy," Stephanie agreed. "At least Sandy will still let us have till the end of our two weeks to shape up."

"That really isn't much time," Darcy said.

"But it is fair," Allie pointed out. "I mean, Sandy is the one in charge of the whole pool. If anyone really gets hurt, she'll be in big trouble."

"And we'll never hear the end of it from Rene," Anna added.

"I'm just glad Austin wasn't really hurt," Allie said.

"And that Sandy knows he wasn't really hurt, too," Kayla added.

"Yeah, she might not believe Rene so fast the next time she says there's a big emergency," Stephanie said. "Anyway, tomorrow is a brand-new day of camp. And I bet it's going to be terrific."

"Well, it's tomorrow," Stephanie said. "And it isn't terrific."

She glanced at the Club Stephanie picnic tables. Only six campers sat there. To Stephanie's surprise, Austin and Tyler had shown up. Two little boys and two little girls also sat at the table. The rest of their campers were across the lawn. They were Little Flamingoes now.

"I'm still amazed that Austin is back at Club Stephanie," Allie whispered.

"Only because he and Tyler are new best friends, and Tyler's mom wouldn't let him switch camps," Darcy whispered back.

Stephanie tried to smile. "Well, let's look on the bright side," she said. "A small group of kids is easier to manage."

"Let's just hope Sandy doesn't see how few campers we have left," Allie replied. "And how many the Flamingoes have."

"But Stephanie's right," Darcy told her. "We

should try to look at the bright side. After all, six kids is better than none."

"I've been thinking," Stephanie began. "We have more than a week of camp left. Maybe we could figure out a way to get our campers back from the Little Flamingoes."

"I guess we could do more glamorous stuff with the girls," Kayla suggested. "You know, like the Flamingoes do."

"But then we'll lose the boys," Allie pointed out.

"Maybe we can find stuff they'll *all* like. Like more games with snacks," Anna said.

"And don't forget the regular camp games, too," Darcy added. "You know—capture the flag and maybe even soccer or Frisbee. And everyone loves playing Marco Polo in the pool."

"Yeah—but we need to make that stuff better," Stephanie said. "Like hold a Marco Polo tournament or something."

"That's a great idea!" Darcy said. "We could do that and offer fun prizes for the winners."

"But what if the Flamingoes copy us? They could give better prizes," Kayla pointed out. "I mean, we'll hand out bubble gum, and they'll give out a trip to Hawaii."

Everyone laughed. "But it's kind of true," Allie said with a sigh. "I hate to admit it, but so far, whatever we do, the Flamingoes do it better."

"If only we could come up with one great idea," Stephanie told her. "Something simple, but super-special, to make all our campers happy. And even get some of them back from Rene."

There was total silence.

"Don't worry," Stephanie finally said. "I'm sure we'll come up with a great idea soon."

"Anyway, Austin is acting like an angel so far," Anna said. "Maybe Rick told him to behave."

"Shhh!" Allie warned at the mention of Rick's name. Everyone glanced at Stephanie to see how she would react.

"It's okay, you guys," Stephanie said. "You can say his name in front of me. I'm not interested in him anymore, anyway."

"I guess you two didn't get to talk yesterday, did you?" Kayla asked.

"After the disaster with Austin at the pool? Hardly," Stephanie replied. "Rick will probably never speak to me again. He probably thinks I pushed Austin on purpose."

"Come on, Steph, don't say that!" Allie exclaimed. "Rick would never believe you're that mean."

"Why not? He barely knows me, and he already told the Flamingoes I act like a baby," Stephanie pointed out.

"But at least you won't have to face him today," Allie said. "Chad and Pete are on lifeguard duty."

"Thank goodness," Stephanie said with relief. She stood up and clapped. "Listen up, campers!" she called. "Let's head to the pool—for a Marco Polo tournament. With prizes!"

"All right!" Austin shouted. He and Tyler slapped each other high fives.

Stephanie gave Allie a thumbs-up sign. They marched their campers to the pool in two short lines, making a game of it. Stephanie turned her head as Sandy walked past. Sandy stared at their small group, but she didn't say anything about how few campers were with them.

"Uh-oh. Here come Rene and the Little Flamingoes," Darcy said. "What are *they* doing at the pool now?"

"I don't know, but I'm going to find out," Stephanie said. She hurried up to Rene. "Hey, you guys aren't supposed to use the pool until after we do."

"Don't worry, we won't," Rene said. Alyssa and the other counselors pushed chairs and tables together. "We're just going to sit here for a while," she said.

"Really?" Stephanie asked. "Sounds boring. Our campers are having a Marco Polo tournament," she bragged. "Watch out—when the Little Flamingoes see how much fun we're having, they might join Club Stephanie.''

Rene laughed. "Oh, I'm not worried," she said. She turned her back and helped get her campers settled.

Stephanie hurried back to her group. Darcy and Kayla were splashing in the water with the kids. Allie and Anna sat with their feet dangling in the water.

"I can't believe that the Little Flamingoes are just sitting there," Darcy said.

"Yeah. I guess Rene and her friends finally ran out of ideas." Stephanie laughed.

Austin yelled from the pool, "Oh, boy, look! Here comes pizza. I hope it's for us!"

A delivery boy headed toward the pool. Boxes of pizza were stacked high in his arms. Stephanie frowned. "That pizza isn't for us," she told Austin. "It's probably for some grown-ups in the clubhouse."

The delivery boy began to yell. "Pizza to Go!" he called. "Where do I find Rene Salter?"

"Right over here," Rene shouted back. "Okay, Little Flamingoes! Time for our poolside pizza party!" Squeals of delight rang out across the pool.

"They're having a pizza party?" Tyler raced up the steps out of the pool. "I'm joining their camp!"

"Me too," Austin said. He raced after him. The other boys and girls followed.

"Wait, guys! You just had snacks!" Stephanie called. None of the campers paid any attention.

Stephanie stared in dismay as the Club Stephanie campers begged Rene for pizza. "Sure, you can have some," Rene told them. "Everybody's welcome at the Little Flamingoes camp!"

Stephanie gazed helplessly at her friends. "Now what?" she asked.

"Now nothing." Darcy sighed as she and Anna climbed out of the pool. "Let's face it, guys. We can't compete with a pizza party."

Allie looked grim. "I can't imagine any special event we could have now."

"Me either," Stephanie said. "But we can't let the Flamingoes win. If only we could come up with that one special idea. One really fun thing to get all our campers back."

"You mean, something like putting on a special show for the whole pool?" Anna asked.

"Exactly!" Stephanie exclaimed. "That's a great idea!"

"I know," Anna told her. "The only trouble is, the Flamingoes thought of it first. Look!"

Stephanie turned to look where Anna was pointing. She saw Alyssa and Tiffany tacking up a big banner on the side of the clubhouse:

PREMIERE OF THE LITTLE FLAMINGOES CHEERLEADERS!
COME ONE, COME ALL!
THURSDAY AT THE POOL!
FOOD AND FUN FOR EVERYONE!

Kayla groaned. "We might as well give up and go home," she said.

"I almost wish we could," Allie agreed.

"Well, you definitely can't leave now, Allie," Darcy told her. "Because Chad is coming right this way."

"Oh, no!" Allie flushed. "I don't want him to see that our camp is a total flop!"

"Too late," Stephanie whispered.

"Hey, Allie. What's up?" Chad asked. He sat beside her. "Why did all your campers get out of the water?"

"Um, they sort of joined Rene's Little Flamingoes," Allie said. "She bought them all pizza. We couldn't compete with that."

"Wow. Too bad," Chad said. "You guys look really down."

"We are," Kayla told him. "We thought camp was going great—and now this." She shook her head.

"You could use some serious cheering up," Chad said. "I know! You should all go to the big summer fair tonight."

91

"What summer fair?" Allie asked.

"It's out by Fisherman's Wharf, on the other side of town," Chad told her.

"I heard about that," Anna said. "My folks said it's going to be like a big, old-fashioned carnival. They said it's mainly for tourists. But I think it sounds like fun."

Chad smiled at Allie. "What do you think, Allie?" he asked.

Allie stared at Chad's bright blue eyes. "It could be fun," she said. "If you went with me," she blurted.

Stephanie nearly choked. Anna poked her in the side. "I can't believe she said that!" Darcy whispered.

Allie had flushed dark red, but she was still looking right at Chad.

Chad's eyes widened. "Are you asking me for a date?"

"I guess so," Allie said. She seemed as surprised as Chad.

"Well, I was planning to check it out tonight," Chad told her. "How about making it a double date? I'll find a friend."

"Sure!" Allie beamed at him. "That sounds great."

"Okay. You're on," Chad said. "You find a friend to come, too. We'll meet you at the main ticket booth at seven-thirty tonight." He jumped to his feet. "I've got to get back on duty now," he said. "But I'll see you later!"

"Later," Allie told him. Chad strolled over to the lifeguard chair. For an instant, there was silence.

"I can't believe you just did that!" Stephanie exclaimed. She stared at Allie in disbelief.

"I don't believe it, either," Allie admitted. "I guess there really *is* a whole new me this summer!"

"A new you that asks boys on dates!" Darcy chuckled. "This is totally amazing."

"Well, I like it," Allie said with her eyes shining. "Except for one thing." Allie grabbed Stephanie's arm. "Steph, you have got to come with me tonight. Say you can double, please?"

"No problem," Stephanie said. "I just hope that Chad's friend is as cute as Chad!"

"Really? You mean it? You'll come?" Allie asked.

"Why not?" Stephanie replied. "There might not be any more Club Stephanie tomorrow," she said. "But who knows? Maybe I'll end up with a brand-new boyfriend instead!"

CHAPTER
11

◆ ◀ ◆ ◆

At seven-thirty, Stephanie and Allie hurried across the street to the carnival entrance. There were colorful, flashing lights everywhere—and the sound of people laughing and screaming on the rides, and the tinkling of merry-go-round music.

Stephanie felt a burst of excitement. "This will be so much fun," she told Allie. "I'm really glad I came."

"Chad said he'd meet us at the ticket booth," Allie said. She peered through the crowd and let out a sigh of relief. "There he is! He actually showed up. Stephanie, I'm so excited!" She squeezed Stephanie's arm as they pushed through the crowd.

"Allie, hi!" Chad called. He beamed at her. "You look great."

"Thanks," Allie said. "But where's your friend? You did bring a friend for Stephanie, didn't you?"

"Sure. He's getting tickets for us," Chad said. "Oh, here he is. Rick—you know Stephanie."

Stephanie's mouth dropped open in shock as Rick appeared, dressed in faded jeans, with his hair freshly combed. "*You're* Chad's friend?" she asked.

"And you're Allie's?" Rick asked back. He turned to glare at Chad.

"What's wrong?" Chad asked. "I told you that Allie was bringing a cool friend."

"Yeah, but you didn't say it was *Stephanie*," Rick replied.

Stephanie felt her cheeks burn in embarrassment.

"I don't get it." Chad seemed confused. "I thought you guys would be happy. I mean, I thought—"

"Allie and I need to talk," Stephanie interrupted. She grabbed Allie's arm and pulled her aside. "Rick?" Stephanie shrieked. "You fixed me up with Rick?"

"I didn't know it was Rick," Allie said.

"This is a total disaster!" Stephanie exclaimed. "Rick hates me!"

"Calm down, Stephanie," Allie begged. "Maybe it's not as bad as that. I mean, you and Rick had some bad luck. But you started out really great. Maybe you could still get together."

"That's impossible." Stephanie shook her head.

Allie sighed. "Listen, Steph, it's only for a few hours," she began. "All you have to do is go on a few rides. You don't even have to talk to Rick if you don't want to."

"No way. I can't go through with this," Stephanie said.

"You have to! Please," Allie pleaded. "I need you here. I can't make it through the night without you! You know how nervous I get around boys."

"The new Allie doesn't get nervous," Stephanie pointed out.

"Yeah, but what if I turn back into the old Allie?" Allie clasped her hands together. "Steph, you can't let me down now. You're my best friend. I'd do it for you!"

Stephanie sighed. "Oh, okay, I guess," she said.

"I'm really, really grateful," Allie told her. She took a deep breath. "Now, do I look all right?"

Stephanie glanced at Allie's light blue T-shirt and black jeans. Over them she wore a denim shirt with a suede collar.

"You look great, Al," Stephanie told her.

"So do you," Allie said. Stephanie was wearing a cropped, bright blue cotton sweater with a pair of new white jeans. "And I love your hair in a french braid," she added.

"Well, I thought I was dressing up to meet some cute new boy," Stephanie said. "I never would have tried to look this nice for Rick."

"Oh, come on, Steph. Admit it—Rick is a pretty cute guy," Allie said. "Very cute, in fact. Though not as cute as Chad," she quickly added.

Stephanie put her hand on Allie's arm. "Listen, Al, don't worry. I won't ruin your big night with Chad. I said I'd go through with this, and I will."

But I didn't say I'd enjoy myself, she added to herself.

Allie led Stephanie back to where the boys were waiting. "All set," she called out.

Chad smiled. "Great. So, what do you say we hit the rides first?" he asked. "I like The Screamer."

Rick shrugged. "Fine with me, if it's okay with Stephanie."

"Why wouldn't it be? Do you think I'm too scared to go or something?" Stephanie demanded.

"I didn't say that." Rick frowned.

Stephanie tossed her head. "Good. So let's hit The Screamer, then."

They headed toward the rides. Stephanie looked up and swallowed hard. The Screamer was a type of roller coaster, made of two huge loops sitting next to each other. Brightly colored cars drove up one side of a loop, hung upside down, and then rushed back down again. Then the cars went on to the next loop and repeated the moves.

Rick stopped to hand in their tickets. "You're sure it doesn't look too scary?" he asked.

"That little thing? I've been on a much scarier ride than that," Stephanie retorted. She crossed her fingers behind her back. Actually, she *had* been on a scarier ride—but she had gotten off before it started. Hanging upside down in an open car high above the ground was *not* her favorite thing.

Allie climbed into an empty car next to Chad. Stephanie and Rick sat in the seat behind them. Stephanie scooted into the corner and glanced at Rick sideways. He sat staring straight ahead. A blond curl spilled onto his forehead.

Stephanie felt a pang of regret. Rick really was cute. And this ride might have been different. If only they had gone on a date *before*—before she found out that Rick thought she was a baby. If only . . .

The Screamer lurched and took off. The cars climbed slowly into the first loop, then speeded up. Stephanie's eyes widened in alarm.

Don't look down, she told herself.

A second later, they were hanging upside down. The car teetered, then plunged downward, moving so fast that Stephanie felt as if her stomach were left behind. She gripped the safety bar tightly. She opened her mouth to scream, but no sound came out—she was holding her breath.

She closed her eyes. *Oh, please, let this be over soon!* she thought.

The car zoomed around the bottom of the loop, suddenly traveling right-side up. Stephanie breathed in relief. But then the car began to climb again. It reached the top of the second loop, hung there, and then dropped down—backward!

Stephanie gasped as she was thrown back against the seat. With a jolt, the car began to climb upward again. Stephanie was thrown forward into the air. She felt as if she would fly right out of the car!

"Eeeaaah!" she heard herself scream. A strong arm shot out and held her safely in the car. Rick! She glanced at him sideways. He was staring straight ahead with a shaky smile across his face.

He's as scared as I am! Stephanie realized. It made her feel a whole lot better.

Finally the ride was over. The cars slid to a stop, and everyone climbed out. Stephanie's legs felt like rubber.

"That was great, huh?" she forced herself to say to Rick.

"Yeah, great," Rick agreed. He paused. "No. Actually, it was pretty scary," he said.

"Really. You think so?" Stephanie asked.

"Yeah. Sitting next to you was scary," Rick joked. "I was afraid you might knock me out of my seat."

Stephanie felt a burst of anger. "Listen, I've had enough of your—" she began.

Rick cut her off. "Wait. I'm sorry," he said. "That was a dumb joke. I didn't mean it."

"You didn't?" Stephanie looked at him in surprise.

"No." Rick frowned. "Maybe we got off on the wrong foot or something. But I—"

Allie interrupted, grabbing Stephanie by the arm. "Come on, hurry," she said. "Chad wants to hit the game booths."

Stephanie hurried behind Allie and Chad, wondering what else Rick meant to say.

"Watch me win Allie a panda bear," Chad said. He herded them all toward a booth where you had to throw darts to burst balloons. The top of the booth was lined with huge, furry stuffed pandas. They were so cute that Stephanie wished she could win one of them for herself.

Chad missed every balloon.

"Hey, let me try to win one, too," Rick said.

Rick paid the man and threw six darts at the balloons. Two darts hit balloons, bursting them.

"Good shot! Now choose your prize," the man said.

Rick pointed at something Stephanie couldn't

see. When he turned around, he dangled a stuffed snake in her face. "For you!" he said.

"Yuck!" Stephanie exclaimed. "A snake?" A little boy was passing by, and Stephanie thrust the snake at him. "Here. You look like a kid who likes snakes," she said.

Rick stared at her. "Why did you do that?" he asked with a hurt look on his face.

"Because I thought . . . the snake wasn't a joke?" Stephanie replied.

Rick looked embarrassed. "No. It was the best prize you could get for breaking two balloons. You have to break ten to get something good, like the panda."

"Oh," Stephanie said. She felt confused. *Is he trying to be nice after all?* she wondered. *What is going on?*

"Let's do the House of Horrors next," Allie said.

"Only if you promise to protect me from the scary things," Chad clowned, bumping playfully into Allie.

Stephanie and Rick followed close behind them. The House of Horrors was bigger than she expected. It was a long, low series of buildings connected by a tunnel. Kids were already piling into the train that rode through the tunnel.

Allie and Chad found two empty seats and

climbed in. Stephanie and Rick had to take seats two cars behind them. The train took off.

Stephanie was aware of Rick sitting close to her in the dark. The cars rode past a few silly lit-up masks and skulls and skeletons. On one side of them, a phony-looking tomb opened and a hand shot out. Then a fake Dracula flapped his cape and made nasty laughing sounds.

Rick imitated the sounds and laughed. "This is really dumb," he whispered.

Stephanie frowned at him. It didn't make sense. When they first arrived at the carnival, Rick acted as if he didn't want to be on a date with her. But then he did nice things—like keeping her safe on The Screamer. And winning her the stuffed snake. Did he like her—or not?

The car turned a sharp corner and a snarling wolf leaped at their car. Stephanie's heart leaped. She let out a nervous giggle. Then the cars plunged down a completely dark section of track. Suddenly big, black fake spiders dropped down from the ceiling onto their heads. Next to her, Rick let out a yelp. He grabbed onto Stephanie's arm and squeezed it tight.

"I hate spiders," he explained.

"They're only pretend. Don't be such a baby!" Stephanie blurted. She flushed in embarrassment. "Sorry," she mumbled.

"That's okay," Rick said. "I know it's dumb. But I really do hate spiders. Even fake ones."

"It's not that—it's just me calling you a baby, when you think *I'm* the baby," Stephanie said.

"What are you talking about?" Rick gave her a puzzled look.

Stephanie squirmed. "Well, you know—Rene told me. How you think I act like a baby or something." She stared down at her hands in her lap.

"I never said that!" Rick protested. "I never said anything *like* that. Why would Rene . . ."

Stephanie stared at him in shock. "You mean, Rene made it up?"

"I guess. I know I would never say that. It isn't true," Rick told her. "In fact, I think you're really mature. Especially the way you handle your campers."

"But . . . what about what happened with Austin?" Stephanie asked. "You didn't think I was mature then!"

Rick seemed uncomfortable. "I wish you'd forget about that," he said. "I shouldn't have yelled at you. Austin can be a real handful sometimes—I know."

"Really?" Stephanie said.

"Yeah. And sometimes I try to protect him a little too much. But there's a reason," Rick went on. "Our mom is an actress, and she's away a lot. Right now she's in a show that's touring to lots of different cities. We're staying with our grandmother, but I still end up looking after Austin a lot."

"I know what that's like," Stephanie told him. "My mom died a long time ago. I have a big family, but I still end up taking care of my little sister and my twin cousins a lot."

"A big family sounds nice to me," Rick said. "I know Austin would be better off with more family around."

"Is that why he acts up so much?" Stephanie asked. "Because he misses your mom?"

"Yeah," Rick said. "It's tough on the little guy."

"But it's nice that you care so much about him," Stephanie said.

Rick shrugged. "I guess." He seemed embarrassed by her compliment.

Stephanie stared at him in the dark.

This is the way I thought he was, she realized. *Sweet and caring.*

Rick suddenly laughed. "Oh. Now I get it," he said. "I couldn't figure out why you were acting so weird all of a sudden."

"You mean, the way I thought everything you said was a dig?" Stephanie asked.

"Yeah. But now it all makes sense," Rick said. "If you thought that I thought . . . what a mess!"

"Yeah. I can't believe Rene tricked me like that," Stephanie declared.

"Tricked both of us, you mean," Rick added.

"I can't believe I fell for it," Stephanie said.

"Listen, I won't tell if you won't," Rick told her. "And I won't tell that you rode The Screamer with white knuckles and your eyes closed, either," he teased.

"Deal," Stephanie said. She held her hand out to shake Rick's hand. He squeezed it and held on to it instead. Stephanie felt her heart do a flip. She was suddenly aware that they were sitting really close together in the dark.

"We almost wrecked our first date," Rick said. "But maybe we can make up for lost time."

Rick leaned close to her, and Stephanie held her breath. Was he going to kiss her?

Stephanie closed her eyes—and felt Rick's lips brush against hers. She wished it could last forever. When she opened her eyes again, she and Rick just sat there, looking happily at each other.

"How about starting this date all over again?" Rick finally said. "Okay with you?"

"That's great with me," Stephanie replied.

Because suddenly, she didn't ever want the evening to end.

CHAPTER
12

◆ ◀ ◆ ◆

"See? I told you it could happen. I knew you and Rick could get together!" Allie beamed at Stephanie as they steered their bikes toward the community center.

"Isn't it great?" Stephanie gave a dreamy sigh. "And it's also great that Rene's little trick failed," she added.

"She is so rotten!" Allie exclaimed. "The way she almost wrecked things for you and Rick—it makes me so mad!"

"Tell me about it," Stephanie replied. She grinned. "I'm just glad that Rick and I straightened it all out."

"I'm glad, too," Allie said. "You like Rick, and

I like Chad—best friends dating friends." She sighed. "We couldn't have planned it any better."

"It's like a miracle," Stephanie said. "You know, once Rick and I really started talking, I found out we have tons in common."

"Same with me and Chad," Allie said. "I didn't have any trouble talking to him at all. He's so funny and nice. We laughed together all night."

"I'm glad the 'new you' is so happy," Stephanie said.

They reached the community center and steered their bikes into the bike rack. Stephanie frowned as she locked up her old bike. "If only this bike were perfect," she said. "I guess I'll never earn enough money to buy a new one now," she added. "Not if Club Stephanie closes."

"I wonder if we'll even have camp today," Allie remarked as they entered the center. They passed the pool and headed toward the picnic area. Stephanie's heart sank. Only Anna, Darcy, and Kayla sat at the Club Stephanie picnic tables. There wasn't a camper in sight.

Anna saw them and waved. At that moment Cynthia Hanson and Tiffany Schroeder walked past on their way to the Little Flamingoes camp.

"Why don't you guys just give up and go home," Cynthia said. She gave them a pitying smile. "Your camp is history."

"Yeah, who wants to belong to Club Stephanie when they can be Little Flamingoes?" Tiffany added. "Our kids do cool stuff. And kids know cool when they see it."

"Really? Most kids don't think being snobs is cool," Stephanie said.

Cynthia opened her mouth to reply, but Allie interrupted. "Stephanie, look!" Tyler, Frederick, and Austin ran up to them.

"We're bored," Tyler said. "We don't want to be dumb cheerleaders anymore."

"Yeah. Little Flamingoes do girl stuff," Frederick added.

Stephanie shot a quick glance at Cynthia. "Oh, really? What do you guys want to do?" Stephanie asked the boys.

"We want to play battle tag," Austin answered. "With our super-squirters. We want to squirt each other."

"That *does* sound cool," Stephanie said. "And kids know what's cool." She smiled at Cynthia and Tiffany.

"Okay, guys, time for battle tag," Allie said. "But wear your bathing suits so your clothes don't get wet."

"All right!" Austin, Frederick, and Tyler gave each other high fives. They took off for the Club Stephanie tables.

Cynthia shrugged. "I guess Club Stephanie *seems* cool to some kids," she said.

"Oh, who cares?" Tiffany sniffed. "Those boys weren't right for the Little Flamingoes, anyway." Cynthia and Tiffany hurried away.

Allie giggled.

"Allie," Stephanie said, "Austin just gave me the most amazing idea! It may be the secret to saving our camp! And it's so simple, you won't believe it."

"What is it?" Allie asked.

Stephanie smiled. "We should let the kids choose what *they* want to do! They can take turns and choose one special thing each day."

"I get it! Like, Austin would choose battle tag," Allie said with growing excitement. "And Kelly would want more face painting, and—"

"And who knows what else they'll come up with?" Stephanie cut in. "That's been our problem all along—not knowing what they like best. But we don't have to guess what they like to do. We can just *ask* them!"

"You're right, Steph. It's so simple, it's brilliant!" Allie slapped Stephanie a high five.

"I have a feeling that Club Stephanie is on its way back," Stephanie said.

She and Allie hurried to tell the others what just happened. Soon Austin, Tyler, and Frederick were leading a super-squirter charge against Kayla and Darcy.

"They're having a great time," Anna said. "They don't even care that Rene's group just went into the clubhouse to watch a Disney video."

"And here come more boys now!" Stephanie exclaimed. Six little boys raced out of the clubhouse and headed toward Club Stephanie.

"We don't want to see a dumb movie about a princess," a boy named Patrick said. "We want to play battle tag, too!"

"Okay," Stephanie told them. She quickly got the boys into the game. Half an hour later, another group of boys ran out of the clubhouse and joined in. Darcy and Anna led the game while Stephanie, Allie, and Kayla took a break.

"This is so fantastic," Allie said to Stephanie. "We've got all the boys back!"

"They're so into this, they won't even stop for a snack," Kayla added.

"Now if we could just get the girls back, Club Stephanie would be saved," Stephanie said.

"Maybe we'll just run a camp for boys," Allie said.

"Oh, I think the girls will come back," Kayla told her. "I mean, how much cheerleading can you do in a summer?"

"We'll find out this afternoon," Stephanie said. "After the Little Flamingoes cheerleading show."

Allie made a face. "I almost forgot about that," she said. "Can we talk about something else?"

"Okay. Let's talk about ice cream! Who wants to hit the mall for sundaes after camp today?" Kayla asked.

"Sorry, Kayla," Stephanie said. "Allie and I are meeting Rick and Chad at the snack shack this afternoon."

"Another double date?" Kayla raised her eyebrows.

"What's this about a date?" Darcy asked. She collapsed onto a picnic bench, out of breath from playing battle tag.

"Stephanie and Allie are meeting Rick and Chad after camp today. They have a double date for lunch," Kayla said.

"That's not all," Stephanie admitted. "We also have a date to go to the movies with them tonight."

"No!" Anna squealed in delight. "That is so cool!"

"The biggest romances of the year, happening right under our noses," Kayla added. "I think we should all have lunch at the snack shack to see what happens next," she teased.

"Don't you dare," Allie told her.

111

"Don't worry. I wouldn't be so mean," Kayla said. Anna agreed.

"Me either," Darcy added. "Besides, after two hours of battle tag, I'm too tired to eat lunch!"

"Steph! Allie!" Chad called across the snack shack. "Over here!"

Stephanie straightened her T-shirt and her flowered skirt. Beside her, Allie ran a hand nervously over her hair.

"Don't worry, you look great," Stephanie whispered to her. She and Allie hurried across the big patio at the snack shack. Chad and Rick had saved them a place in line at the food counter.

Stephanie glanced shyly at Rick. *What if he doesn't like me today?* she wondered.

Rick's eyes lit up when he saw her. Stephanie grinned. He *definitely* liked her!

They ordered sandwiches and drinks and took them to a table near the entrance.

"Club Stephanie camp seemed to go great today," Rick said. "When I looked over, all the kids were having a blast."

Stephanie nodded. "Yeah, we finally got the hang of it," she said. "Most of our boys came back."

"But the girls are still in the Little Flamingoes,"

Allie added. "They're all excited about the big cheerleading show this afternoon."

"Not as excited as I am about our movie date tonight," Rick said. "You two still want to go out with us, right?"

"Absolutely," Stephanie told him.

"Right!" Allie said. She and Chad smiled happily at each other.

"Excuse me. Did I hear someone mention going out tonight?"

Stephanie looked up. Rene and Alyssa were standing beside their table.

"Hi, Rick. Hi, Chad," Rene said, ignoring Stephanie and Allie. "We just came over to remind you about the party tonight," she said.

"Party?" Rick gave her a blank look. Then his eyes narrowed. "Is this another one of your stories?" he demanded. "Like telling Stephanie some story about me, saying I said that she was a baby?"

Wow! Stephanie thought. *Way to go, Rick!* She glanced at Allie, who gave her a thumbs-up sign.

Rene's cheeks flushed bright red. "That was no story," she insisted. "Someone *told* me you said that."

"Listen, whatever Rene said, it doesn't matter now," Stephanie told Rick. "Right?" She smiled at him, and he grinned back at her.

"Right," Rick said.

"Rene is so jealous!" Allie whispered to Stephanie.

Rene tossed her head. "Anyway, the party tonight is no story," she said. "It's the big lifeguards' cookout. They told us about it at our last meeting. Remember?"

"Oh, no." Rick turned to Stephanie and Allie. "She's right! There is a cookout tonight—but I forgot all about it."

"Me too," Chad added.

"So I guess you can't go on any dates tonight," Alyssa said. "But don't worry—we'll have lots of fun at our cookout. Lifeguards only, of course," she added with a smirk.

"Steph, I'm sorry," Rick said. "The whole lifeguard staff has to go to this thing."

"It'll be great," Alyssa went on. "We're going to have a barbecue and stay out really late—way after the pool is closed. It'll be very romantic," she finished, looking right at Chad.

"Anyway, we just wanted to remind you," Rene said. "We have to hurry now. It's time for the last rehearsal of our cheerleading show." She looked at Rick. "You are coming to the show, aren't you, Rick?"

"And you too, Chad," Alyssa added.

Rick frowned. "How could we miss it?" he asked. "We're both on duty at the pool this afternoon. We'll be right across from the clubhouse when you have the show."

"Well, good. Then you'll be able to see everything." Rene gave him a quick nod. "So we'll see you guys tonight, then," she said. She and Alyssa hurried away.

"Thanks for sticking up for me," Stephanie said quietly to Rick. "You know, about the 'baby' business."

"No problem," Rick told her. "Like you said, it doesn't matter now, anyway." He glanced at the big clock hanging over the food counter. "Wow, it's late. We have to get back to work," he said. "Come on, Chad."

Chad stood up. "Well, see you around the pool," he told Allie.

"See you," Allie replied. She smiled as he walked away. But as soon as he was gone, she grabbed Stephanie's arm. "Did you see that?" she shrieked.

"See what?" Stephanie asked, feeling confused.

"The way Alyssa was looking at Chad!" Allie exclaimed. "I think she likes him!"

"No way," Stephanie said. "Besides, Chad likes you. Everyone knows that. You have nothing to worry about."

"Oh, yeah? Chad might like me now," Allie said.

"But wait till Alyssa gets him alone tonight! Anything could happen."

"Allie, that's crazy," Stephanie told her. "Chad won't suddenly forget about you. He could have asked Alyssa out before this—*if* he liked her. Really."

"I guess," Allie said, but she didn't sound very sure.

"Hey, you're forgetting one thing," Stephanie told her. "Rene and Alyssa just heard Rick and Chad ask us out on dates."

"So?" Allie asked.

"So I think that was about the best moment of my life," Stephanie said. "After that, who cares about some dumb cookout?"

CHAPTER
13

♦ ◂ ▸ ♦

"Check this out," Stephanie said. She and Allie had just met Kayla, Darcy, and Anna outside the clubhouse. It was almost time for the Little Flamingoes cheerleading show. Rows of chairs were lined up across the lawn.

"There must be a hundred chairs," Allie said in surprise. "They really expect a big crowd."

"And they might get one, too," Darcy told her. She nodded toward the entrance to the pool. Groups of people were already beginning to push through the turnstile.

"Stephanie!" Sandy appeared in the clubhouse doorway. She strode past the rows of chairs, heading toward their group.

"Oh, no." Stephanie groaned. "I can't believe Sandy is coming to talk to us *now*. Just when the Flamingoes are pulling in an enormous crowd."

Kayla, Darcy, Allie, and Anna glanced at the crowd. It was getting larger by the minute. More and more people were arriving. Proud parents and brothers and sisters milled about, eagerly chatting with one another.

"Look at all the families here! This proves that their camp is a huge hit," Stephanie said. "I mean, suppose we had a show? With so few campers, we'd probably have twelve people in the audience."

"I guess our camp seems pretty pathetic compared to this," Kayla admitted.

They all stared miserably as Sandy approached them.

"Hi, girls," Sandy called in a cheerful voice. "Isn't this exciting?" She glanced at the crowd. "This is exactly the kind of event I was hoping we could manage," she said. "This shows the whole community how valuable the pool is to them. And it proves we were right about starting a camp here—there is a real need for it. And tons of support."

"It certainly shows all that," Stephanie agreed, trying to sound upbeat herself.

"Yes." Sandy's smile faded. "Of course, this makes my decision a little harder."

"Decision?" Stephanie repeated. She exchanged a look of alarm with Allie, Darcy, Anna, and Kayla.

"Yes. Things haven't worked out exactly as I hoped," Sandy went on. "I thought you and the Flamingoes would work together. But I see that's not going to happen."

"We tried to get along with them," Darcy began to protest. "But they—"

Sandy held up a hand to stop her. "It's okay," Sandy said. "I guess I expected too much." She paused. "Still, it's clear to me that we can only have one camp here. I'll have to decide who runs it."

Stephanie felt her stomach drop. "B-but we can work things out, Sandy," she said.

"Sure! We can learn to get along with the Flamingoes, especially if we really have to," Anna added.

"Is that so?" Sandy raised an eyebrow, giving Anna a doubtful look. "You haven't tried much so far."

"Of course not," Anna went on. "Like you said, it takes time for new arrangements to work. And we did cooperate with Rene for the cheerleading show," she added.

"You did? How?" Sandy asked.

"Simple," Anna replied. "We let Rene handle the kids who wanted to learn cheers while we took care of the kids who *didn't* want to learn them!" Anna beamed at Sandy.

I almost believe that myself, Stephanie thought, grinning.

"Actually, I guess you *did* do that. But not exactly on purpose, right?" Sandy asked.

The girls exchanged looks. "Not exactly," Anna admitted.

"I'm sorry," Sandy said. "I don't like having to choose between you. But Club Stephanie has five counselors—and six campers. That's not a camp," she said. "That's baby-sitting. Which is not what the community center wants to offer."

"But you don't have to choose between us," Stephanie told her. "Not yet. We still have one more week, plus one day of our trial period. You can't close down our camp before that. It wouldn't be fair."

"That's true," Darcy said at once. Allie, Anna, and Kayla nodded.

Sandy held up her hands. "Okay, okay. I'll let you finish your trial period," she said. "But only because I promised."

"We understand," Stephanie said. "And we agree—if Club Stephanie can't get more campers, we'll close at the end of next week. But we won't give up a minute before then!"

Sandy grinned. "I admire your fighting spirit," she said. "Good luck." She hurried off to greet a group of parents.

Stephanie let out a long sigh. "That was rough," she said.

"But you were great, Steph," Kayla told her.

"So were you, Anna," Allie said, laughing. "You almost had me believing that we were getting rid of campers on purpose."

Anna chuckled. "Thanks—I tried," she said. "I know I haven't been part of this group for very long. But I don't want to see Club Stephanie end. You guys are great. And we're great together!"

"Definitely," Kayla agreed. "I feel exactly the same way."

"Well, one thing's for sure," Stephanie told them. "We may not have a camp very much longer. But we made some great new friends in you and Kayla."

"Oh, thank you!" Anna threw her arms around Stephanie and gave her a giant hug. Everybody started laughing.

"Hey, Anna—sorry to break this up," Darcy said. "But if we want to see the show, we'd better grab seats before they're all gone!"

"Yikes!" Stephanie said, glancing at the crowd. "The only empty chairs are in the back row."

"That's fine with me," Allie said. "I don't want to be too near the Flamingoes, anyway."

Allie and Anna hurried toward the back row of chairs. The others followed. Stephanie had turned to go when Rene suddenly appeared at her side.

"Just a minute," Rene told Stephanie, pulling her aside.

"Now what, Rene?" Stephanie asked. "Don't you have a show to put on?"

"It can wait one second," Rene said. She crossed her arms and scowled. "You really think Rick likes you, don't you?" she asked.

"I know he does," Stephanie said. "And so do you." She tried to walk away, but Rene grabbed her again.

"Not after tonight," Rene said.

Stephanie frowned. "What are you talking about?" she demanded.

Rene shrugged. "You know. Once he's had a date with me, you'll be history."

"If you mean the cookout tonight, that's not a date," Stephanie pointed out. "Even you said it— Rick *has* to go. And he didn't choose to go with you."

"Maybe not. But just wait and see what happens

after I get him alone. And then don't say I didn't warn you." Rene smiled. "Enjoy the show!" She hurried up to the cleared space in front of the clubhouse.

She's bluffing, Stephanie told herself. *Rick likes me. I know Rick likes me. I have absolutely nothing to worry about. Right?*

CHAPTER
14

◆ ◄ ◆ ◆

"Hello, parents and friends," Rene called to the audience. "Welcome to the Little Flamingoes' first show!"

There was a burst of applause.

"Thank you," Rene said. "We Flamingoes think that performing in public is a great skill for any child to learn. And we think performing cheers is something all little girls love. We taught our campers some of our favorites. We hope you like them, too." She stepped to one side, and twelve little girls ran onto the stage area. They were dressed in matching pink shorts and carried bright pink pom-poms.

"Here they are!" Rene called. "The Little Flamingoes cheerleaders!"

The audience oohed and aahed.

"I have to admit, they do look cute," Stephanie whispered to Allie.

Rene nodded, and the kids began to chant.

"We're the Flamingoes, and no one could be prouder," they yelled. Eleven girls stepped forward—and one stepped sideways and dropped her pom-pom. The audience laughed.

"Wait!" Rene called. She leaped in front of her campers. "Start over! And this time, get it right," she scolded the girls. She waited for the girls to line up again. Then she flashed the audience a big smile and nodded at the girls to begin.

"We're the Flamingoes, and—" Kelly and Trisha bumped into each other. "Hey, you did it wrong!" Kelly exclaimed. Trisha pouted.

The audience laughed again as Rene ran out and separated Trisha and Kelly. "Stay in line, Trisha," she snapped. "We're going to start over, everyone!" Rene called brightly to the audience. She nodded, and the girls began.

The girls on the right called out, "Yell a little louder!" The girls on the left yelled, "And if you don't believe us . . ." Both groups of girls stopped in confusion. They stared at one another.

"No, no, no!" Rene shrieked. "You're getting everything wrong! Start from the beginning—now!"

Trisha burst into tears and ran off the stage.

"Well, don't just start crying!" Rene exclaimed in disgust.

"Hey, take it easy! They're only little kids," Trisha's mother declared. She rushed up to Trisha and threw her arms around her. "It's okay, sweetheart," she said. She led Trisha away.

Suddenly Kelly started crying, too. She ran to *her* mother in the audience.

"Wait! Stop it! Where are you going?" Rene shrieked as Jennifer, Kara, and Rebecca ran off the stage. "Alyssa, do something!" Rene yelled.

Alyssa took off, chasing Jennifer. Rene chased after Alyssa. Jennifer saw them both coming and ran faster. She spotted Stephanie in the crowd and raced over to her.

"Help, Stephanie!" Jennifer shrieked. "I hate the Little Flamingoes! I want to be in Club Stephanie again!"

"Me too!" Kara added, running up to Stephanie. "Those big Flamingoes yell too much!"

"Well, sure, you can be in Club Stephanie again," Stephanie said. She hugged Jennifer and Kara. She looked up at her friends and grinned.

"This is too much," Rene declared angrily. "I give up." She stormed into the clubhouse. Alyssa ran after her. Two of the Little Flamingoes tried to start the cheers over again, but the others fled into the audience. The last two Little Flamingoes gave up and also ran into the audience. There was a lot of noise and confusion as everyone got up to leave.

Tiffany ran to the stage area. "Uh—I guess the show's over. Thanks for coming," she called to the crowd. Two or three parents applauded.

Stephanie chuckled. "Amazing. That was a total flop!"

"Finally—the Flamingoes lose and we win!" Darcy exclaimed.

"The best part is that Sandy saw the whole thing," Anna added. "I bet she never saw the 'real' Rene before. She must have been pretty surprised!" Anna laughed.

Allie wasn't smiling. "Yeah. But now Rene will hate us more than ever," she said with a grim expression. "And if I know her, she'll find a way to make us pay."

"Oh, who cares about the Flamingoes now?" Darcy asked. "No matter what happens next week, at least they flopped today."

"And they flopped big time!" Anna giggled. "I couldn't have planned it better myself!"

"Darcy's right," Stephanie said. "This may be the best moment of our whole summer. We should enjoy it while it lasts."

"I feel so good, I want to celebrate," Kayla said. Her eyes lit up. "I know! Let's all go to my house tonight! We can have the first ever Club Stephanie counselors' sleepover!"

"Perfect! That's such a great idea, Kayla," Stephanie agreed. "We'll have a blast—and forget all about the Flamingoes!"

"Okay, I have a special surprise, as soon as we get to my room," Kayla said as she led the way up the stairs.

"This is a fantastic house," Stephanie told her.

Kayla lived in a neighborhood filled with big, old stucco houses. They were painted in bright, light colors. Kayla's house was yellow with pale pink trim around the windows. Her room was the same shade of pale yellow.

"So, what's the surprise?" Darcy asked.

Kayla grinned. She opened a bureau drawer and took out four tiny blue boxes. "These!" she said, handing one box to each of them.

"Charm bracelets!" Stephanie exclaimed. "These are great!" She lifted a delicate gold chain. Attached to the chain was a charm with her name engraved on it.

Allie, Anna, and Darcy tried on their bracelets. Kayla took hers from her jewelry box and fastened it around her wrist.

"Thank you," Anna said. "These are great, Kayla. But how come you got them for us?"

Kayla beamed. "Well, meeting you all has made this summer special already. I love being part of Club Stephanie! I just had to do something to make our first sleepover one we would all remember."

"We will remember it, Kayla!" Stephanie gave her a big hug.

"Yeah, who could forget such a cool kid who has such a cool room?" Anna teased.

"It *is* a cool room," Stephanie agreed. "And you're really lucky you don't have to share it with your sister, Stacy," Stephanie went on.

"I know," Kayla said. "Though Stacy's pretty cool."

"I loved that special pizza she picked up for us," Darcy said.

"Well, she loves having her own car," Kayla said. "She'll drive anyone anywhere, anytime."

Anna was sorting through the stack of videos on Kayla's desk. "Wow! You have some real classics here," she said. "I don't know which to watch first!"

"Allie loves all those old movies," Stephanie said. "She's probably seen them three times each. Which one is the best, Allie?" she asked.

Allie stared out the window.

"Allie?" Stephanie repeated. "Hello . . . anyone home?"

"Oh! What did you say?" Allie whipped her head around.

"What were you thinking about?" Darcy demanded. "You were a million miles away!"

"Not quite," Allie said. "I was just wondering what's going on at the cookout right now."

"Try not to think about it," Stephanie told her.

"Right. It won't do any good to worry," Kayla added.

"I can't help it," Allie said. "I can't stand imagining the worst. I wish I knew what was happening with Alyssa." She paused. "Tell me you're not worried that Rick is there with Rene," she added.

Stephanie felt a pang of worry, but she shrugged it off. "Not really," she replied.

"Well, I'm worried." Allie sighed. "If only we could spy on them or something. But I guess there's no way we could do that."

"Why not?" Darcy asked. "Kayla just said Stacy will drive anywhere. Why not ask her for a ride to the cookout?"

Allie's eyes brightened. She turned to Kayla. "Would she take us?"

"I guess," Kayla said. "If that's what you really want to do."

"It's better than watching old movies and feeling sick to my stomach," Allie replied.

"Steph? How about you?" Kayla asked. The others all turned to look at Stephanie.

"Well, I guess I wouldn't say no," Stephanie admitted.

"Okay. I'll ask Stacy." Kayla stuck her head out the bedroom door. "Hey, Stace!" she yelled down the hall. "You up here?"

A moment later, Kayla's older sister, Stacy, stuck her head around the door. She looked like a taller version of Kayla, slim and pretty with long blond hair. "Yeah, I'm here," Stacy said. "Why? What's up?"

"We need a ride," Kayla told her. "Could you take us somewhere?"

Stacy grinned. She reached into her jeans pocket and took out a set of car keys. She dangled the keys in front of them. "Are you kidding? Here I am with a whole car to myself and nowhere to go. Let's ride!"

"All right!" Anna cheered.

Fifteen minutes later, Stacy pulled her car into the parking lot at the community center. Stephanie could feel her heart beating fast. She had to admit that she was glad Allie thought of spying on the cookout. She was dying to know what was happening between Rick and Rene. *Though nothing is happening, of course,* she told herself.

"Let's peek through the hedges around the outside of the community center," Allie said. "That way, no one will see us watching."

They left Stacy with the car and hurried around the outside of the hedges. Allie giggled nervously as they crept toward the picnic area. "Look, you guys!" Allie parted the branches of the hedges. Straight ahead was the glow of a campfire. "There they are," Allie whispered.

Stephanie could see a group of shadowy figures ahead. Most of the lifeguards were gathered around one of the tables, joking and laughing. Another smaller group sat around the campfire. The firelight glowed on their faces.

Stephanie suddenly recognized Chad's dark, wavy hair—and Alyssa's long blond hair, blowing in the wind. It took her a second to realize that Chad had his arm around Alyssa's shoulders.

"Uh, maybe this wasn't such a good idea," Stephanie quickly said to Allie. "Really. Let's go, and—"

Allie gasped. "Oh, no!" she exclaimed, staring straight at Chad and Alyssa.

"Listen, Al, don't worry," Stephanie said. "Maybe he's, uh, just being friendly or something."

"Right!" Darcy added. "Or maybe Alyssa was cold and he was nice enough to warm her up, or—"

"Oh, sure," Allie said. She ducked her head and

took a deep breath. When she looked up, her eyes were shiny with tears. "I wish we never came here! Let's go. I can't stay another second!"

Allie hurried back toward the parking lot. Anna and Kayla went with her.

"What a disaster!" Darcy told Stephanie. "Now I am sorry that we came."

"Me too," Stephanie replied. "But I wish we didn't have to leave."

"I know, because you wanted to see what Rick was doing, too, didn't you?" Darcy asked.

"Yeah." Stephanie shook herself. "I guess that's silly. I mean, what am I so afraid of, anyway? He's probably just sitting at the table, talking with the other lifeguards."

She swung away from the hedges—and heard a short, high giggle.

"Wait!" Stephanie exclaimed. "That's Rene—I'd recognize that laugh anywhere."

"Great! This is our chance to see what she's up to," Darcy said.

Stephanie crept close to the hedges again. She peered through the darkness. She saw Rene hurrying away from the group at the picnic table. She was pulling someone by the hand.

Rick!

Stephanie gasped. *Oh, no! It can't be!*

Darcy grasped her arm. "Hey, don't get upset,"

she whispered. "It's not like with Chad and Alyssa. I mean, Rick doesn't have his arm around Rene. It's probably nothing."

"It doesn't look like nothing," Stephanie replied.

"Sure it does," Darcy told her. "Rene probably made Rick go with her. And, um, they're probably just going to get something. Like, more marshmallows for the table, or more sodas."

"You really think so?" Stephanie asked.

"Sure," Darcy told her.

Darcy's probably right, Stephanie told herself. *I'm probably getting all worked up over nothing.*

Up ahead, Rick and Rene stopped walking. Rick bent toward Rene. It looked as if—

Stephanie held her breath. She saw Rene turn her face toward Rick's. Rick bent even closer.

Stephanie felt her heart stop. *Please don't*, she silently begged.

Rick's lips brushed against Rene's.

Rick straightened up. Rene laughed, gazing up into his eyes.

I think I'm going to die, Stephanie thought.

"Oh, no. Oh, Steph! You were right," Darcy blurted out. "Coming here was a really, really bad idea."

Stephanie swiped blindly at the tears that suddenly filled her eyes. "I can't believe it," she said. "I trusted him!"

"I'm sorry, Steph," Darcy murmured.

Stephanie squared her shoulders. "No—I can't let this happen," she declared. "I *won't* let Rene ruin everything! I won't!"

"But what can you do?" Darcy asked.

"I don't know," Stephanie told her. "But this isn't the end, Darcy. I'm going to do something. And when I do, Rene better watch out!"

Rene stole Rick! Can Stephanie steal him back— and put Rene in her place, once and for all?

Read FULL HOUSE/CLUB STEPHANIE #2, *Fireworks and Flamingoes* to find out!

ᚈULL HOUSᴇ™
Stephanie

PHONE CALL FROM A FLAMINGO	88004-7/$3.99
THE BOY-OH-BOY NEXT DOOR	88121-3/$3.99
TWIN TROUBLES	88290-2/$3.99
HIP HOP TILL YOU DROP	88291-0/$3.99
HERE COMES THE BRAND NEW ME	89858-2/$3.99
THE SECRET'S OUT	89859-0/$3.99
DADDY'S NOT-SO-LITTLE GIRL	89860-4/$3.99
P.S. FRIENDS FOREVER	89861-2/$3.99
GETTING EVEN WITH THE FLAMINGOES	52273-6/$3.99
THE DUDE OF MY DREAMS	52274-4/$3.99
BACK-TO-SCHOOL COOL	52275-2/$3.99
PICTURE ME FAMOUS	52276-0/$3.99
TWO-FOR-ONE CHRISTMAS FUN	53546-3/$3.99
THE BIG FIX-UP MIX-UP	53547-1/$3.99
TEN WAYS TO WRECK A DATE	53548-X/$3.99
WISH UPON A VCR	53549-8/$3.99
DOUBLES OR NOTHING	56841-8/$3.99
SUGAR AND SPICE ADVICE	56842-6/$3.99
NEVER TRUST A FLAMINGO	56843-4/$3.99
THE TRUTH ABOUT BOYS	00361-5/$3.99
CRAZY ABOUT THE FUTURE	00362-3/$3.99

Available from Minstrel® Books Published by Pocket Books

FULL HOUSE™
Michelle

#1: THE GREAT PET PROJECT 51905-0/$3.50

#2: THE SUPER-DUPER SLEEPOVER PARTY
51906-9/$3.50

#3: MY TWO BEST FRIENDS 52271-X/$3.99

#4: LUCKY, LUCKY DAY 52272-8/$3.50

#5: THE GHOST IN MY CLOSET 53573-0/$3.99

#6: BALLET SURPRISE 53574-9/$3.99

#7: MAJOR LEAGUE TROUBLE 53575-7/$3.50

#8: MY FOURTH-GRADE MESS 53576-5/$3.99

#9: BUNK 3, TEDDY, AND ME 56834-5/$3.99

#10: MY BEST FRIEND IS A MOVIE STAR!
(Super Edition) 56835-3/$3.99

#11: THE BIG TURKEY ESCAPE 56836-1/$3.50

#12: THE SUBSTITUTE TEACHER 00364-X/$3.99

#13: CALLING ALL PLANETS 00365-8/$3.50

#14: I'VE GOT A SECRET 00366-6/$3.99

A MINSTREL® BOOK
Published by Pocket Books